Don't Call Me Coach

by Tagenar

Don't Call Me Coach

Production copyright FurPlanet Productions © 2015

Copyright © Tagenar 2015

Cover Artwork © Linkin Monroe 2015
http://www.furaffinity.net/user/linkinmonroe

Interior Artwork © Nudog 2015
http://www.furaffinity.net/user/Nudog

Published by FurPlanet Productions
Dallas, Texas
www.FurPlanet.com

ISBN 978-1-61450-256-2

Printed in the United States of America
First Edition Trade Paperback 2015

Table of Contents

For Montgomery High, the new principal, and the board of directors. Vengeance is mine.

Special thanks to Nudog for suggesting a setting I could work with, and Ajax for pointing out the obvious mistakes a writer never sees.

Chapter 1

"Mister Hood, your qualifications are stellar."

Garth sat on the opposite side of the desk, hands in his lap, biceps puckering his chest muscles. He was dressed in business casual, sans tie, and he had deliberately worn a shirt one size too small for him. He had done this for the last five places he interviewed, and he couldn't believe he was trying to use his body to get an edge. He figured if females could show a little chest to get ahead in the world, it would work for him, too.

The poodle behind the desk had barely looked at him, which Garth thought was a good sign, as it meant she had noticed and was trying to focus on business and not his cleavage.

"Thank you," Gath said.

"The school year starts in two weeks. We don't like to hire this close to the first day, but we have a vacancy in the gym department."

Garth didn't blink.

"I recognize it may not be what you're after but..."

Gym, Garth thought.

"...there could be many opportunities to grow from here."

Gym.

"We do require our gym coaches to come to the classroom for a few periods a day and teach academic courses, but that won't be a problem for you I'm sure."

Gym?

"You'd be perfect, Mister Hood. You're somebody who can jump into it, and I think the pups would respect you. Are you interested?"

Fuck no! Garth thought.

"I could do that," Garth said.

"Great," said the poodle. Garth couldn't remember her name, only that she was the gatekeeper to his entire future and she probably didn't know it.

She lowered the papers she was holding to the desk and let them drop. She picked up a folder on the side of the desk, pulled a thin stack of papers from it and slid them over to Garth, right-side up from his point of view.

"All the information is here, including salary. You will have students ranging from ninth to twelfth grade. Be ready to start next week. That will only give you a week to prepare for the first day of school. Short notice, I know, but the other coaches will help you out. Have you held a teaching position before, Mister Hood?"

The mastiff leaned forward, plastic chair twisting under his weight. The motion also pushed his biceps and pectorals even further out, and all of a sudden he resented his choice of wardrobe.

These were employment papers. After all the interviews, and the countless applications he had filed but had not interviewed for, he was finally staring at a job. Written right there on the form was the position: Gym Coach. Garth exhaled.

"No," he said. "This will be my first."

The canine in charge of personnel leaned forward on the desk and began talking. Garth didn't hear a word she said. He merely picked up the pen, skimmed over the terms of employment, and signed the papers.

Gym... He thought the word over and over.

When the last paper had ink on it, Garth stood, but the poodle did not. She shook paws with him, and Garth walked out of the office, wishing he had not worn this shirt.

Garth walked to the car, climbed in the seat and held a death grip on the steering wheel. Every muscle north of the waist was tense and flexed. He turned the key, pulled out of the spot and merged into the city traffic. He stopped at a red light at the intersection.

Gym!

Green light. Garth punched the gas three times harder than he needed to and slammed on the brakes as he approached the red light at the next block.

GYM!

Light after light the word kept spinning around in his mind. He bared his teeth and clenched the steering wheel harder. The shirt stretched and strained more and more until finally something popped.

Garth heard it and looked down at his arm. Sure enough his bicep had split the shirt sleeve lengthwise about four inches. The mastiff growled at it. He hated this shirt anyway, but the poodle did say she thought the pups would respect him, so in that sense, this shirt had gotten him the job.

A few lights later, Garth pulled into a strip mall and sped into a parking space. He opened the glove box, removed a pair of shorts from it, and slammed the car door. He walked into his gym, showed his membership card and walked straight to the locker room.

It was empty, and Garth sat on the bench, arms on his thighs. He stared at the floor for a few minutes as he thought the word over and over. He had no steering wheel to crush, so he clenched his fists, twisted his face in a building growl. Finally he snarled and grabbed the shirt and ripped it off, the buttons popped free and rolled everywhere on the floor, and he threw it across the room into the trash can. Garth rested his forearms on his thighs and stared between his pecs at the floor again.

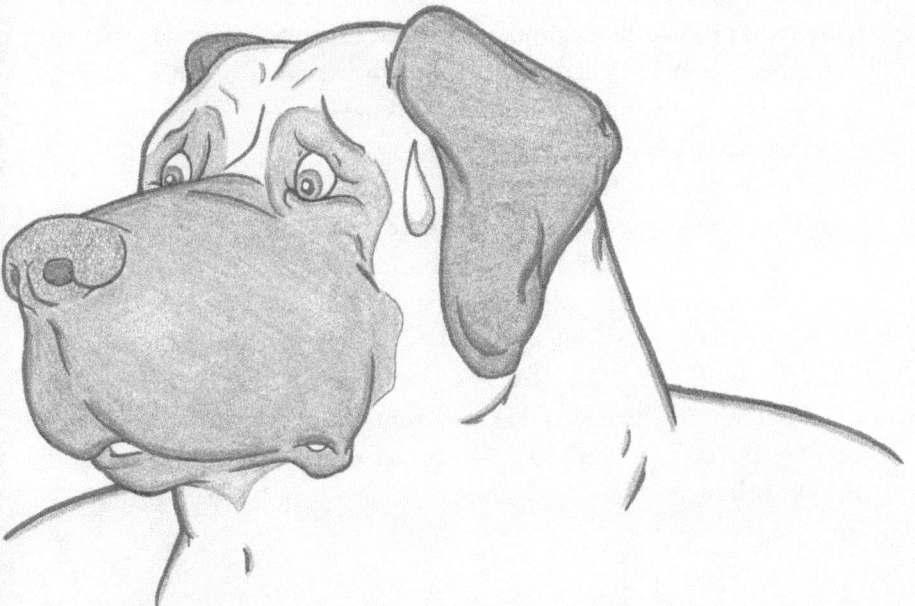

After a few deep breaths, he stood up, undid his pants and carefully took them off. The shirt was no loss, but these pants actually fit him and he didn't want to shop around for another pair. Since he was the only one in the room, he removed them entirely and sat naked in the locker room.

"The pups will respect you," he said.

Garth stood up, flexed his arms, his legs, and his chest, raised his arms and stretched his lats. Then he slipped the shorts on and walked away from the lockers, carrying his pants with him.

Being so early in the morning, the weight room was almost empty. Only three other canines were in here, and they were busy with their own things, so Garth had his free choice of where to do his routine. He picked the bench furthest away from the other patrons and loaded the barbell with a pyramid of plates that was his maximum bench.

He lay under the barbell and benched. It felt too light. He pumped it again and again, faster and harder than he ever had before. He panted severely, letting it disturb his rhythm.

"I'm a fucking gym coach!"

He exhausted his pectorals, sat up and immediately walked to the dumbbells, leaving his pants by the bench. He picked up one of the heaviest the gym had, sat down on the nearest perch and hoisted it over his head with one arm. He worked his triceps next, glancing at the other patrons. They were far enough away not to hear him, so he bared his teeth and growled under his breath.

"Ten years in university." One rep.

"Graduate... twelfth in my class." Two reps.

"I'm a goddamned... scientist!" Three reps.

"I know... how to send people... to Mars and back!"

He worked the next three reps silently, and then switched arms.

"Two years... Looking... for a job... For two years... I have a physics... doctorate! Now... I'm a fucking gym coach!"

Triceps were exhausted. He rose from this bench, set the weight back on the rack and walked to the preacher curl bench. He loaded the barbell with a large pyramid, sat down and began curling, growling.

"I can look... at a goddamned star... and tell you what it's made of... and how far away it is! I can figure out... how much a beam of light bends... as it goes around it! Now I'm teaching... gym!"

He had squeezed twelve repetitions out of that, and now his arms were thoroughly exhausted. He stood up, walked around. Two of the other canines in the room were staring at him. Garth just realized he hadn't done a good job keeping his disgust to himself. It was also a slight breath of etiquette to work out without a shirt like this, but he was twice as big as all of them, and if any of them had a problem with it, they didn't say so.

Garth growled less and less as he moved through his upper body routine. By the time he concluded with shoulders, he felt like he was ready to accept what had happened. Back in the locker room, Garth changed into pants and walked to the door.

He paused at the trash can and peered inside. His button-less shirt was the only piece of garbage in it. He sighed, felt his chest across and down to the forearm. He had never worked out in anger like that before, and his pump was enormous. That muscle pump had made his arms huge, his chest thicker, his shoulders even felt wider and the separation between the muscles was more pronounced than ever. He was a little self-conscious about flashing it now. He reached in, pulled the shirt out and draped it over his shoulders. His arms did not fit in the sleeves and they strained the fabric even more. It would never fit now after this workout, but at least it attempted to cover him. He left the locker room, walked by the front desk and out the door.

Chapter 2

The mastiff turned the handle and pushed the door inward. Conversation did not stop when he poked his head through the door, which was a good sign. It was a generic meeting room with a couple long tables down the middle and chairs arranged around them. He had been told to be here today at nine in the morning for an important meeting between the teachers in his department.

Papers were strewn about, coffee cups were everywhere, and a couple boxes of donuts lay open around the table. There were eight other people in the room, all but one of them were canines.

Garth stepped inside and sat down in a chair next to one of the canines. Garth's scent disturbed the air in the room, and finally everyone noticed him and the chitchat stopped.

"Oh, you must be Garth," said the largest dog in the room, also a mastiff, but with much darker fur. He stood up and offered his paw. Garth rose halfway out of his seat, reached over a box of donuts and shook it. "I'm Terrance."

"Garth Hood," he said. "Just hired last week."

"I heard they finally decided to fill the position last minute," Terrance said.

He let go of Garth's paw and took his seat again. Garth took a seat as well. He was wearing appropriate-fitting clothes this time, going out of his way to avoid showing his time in the gym.

"I'm kind of the informal head of the department," Terrance continued. "No title. Vice principal wants minor issues to come to my attention first so he isn't overwhelmed."

"Sure," Garth said. "So what are we doing?"

"Meeting doesn't start for another ten minutes," said one of the other canines sitting three seats down. He was a collie, probably weighed as much as Garth, but in fat and water. "We've just been chillin' in here for now."

"Right."

"You new to this area?" said a female voice.

Gath's eyes were instantly drawn to the smallest person in the room, a shepherd mixed with collie. Her face was all black but her paws were golden brown. She actually looked like she could be teaching gym.

"Actually yeah, I moved here as part of the job hunt, Ms. ..."

Terrance interrupted. "Oh, if you're new here we should introduce ourselves." He gestured to the female.

"Sasha Grace," said the fit canine. "I'm one of the swim team coaches. I also teach algebra and pre-calc."

The feline with brown fur was Jeremy. He was one of the soccer coaches, and he also taught chemistry. He smelled of cigarette smoke. Garth could hear his emphysema from here as well.

The collie was Vern. When he wasn't coaching tennis, he also taught trigonometry. His fur lacked any kind of sheen, and his eyes were dark. He looked like he lived on cereal and diet soda.

The overweight husky was Joey, who managed the wrestling team and also taught physics and earth science.

The fox was Bob, the other wrestling coach who also taught a health class. He was even more overweight than Joey.

The Rottweiler was Paul. He coached football and also taught health and nutrition. Garth smelled alcohol on his fur, and he was munching on a donut from a nearly-empty box on the table.

The retriever was Gary, who coached one of the gymnastics teams as well as taught social studies. He wasn't obese, but he also didn't look like he could do a cartwheel, much less a backflip.

That brought the introductions back to Terrance. "And I coach the basketball teams, plus I teach economics."

Garth couldn't stop looking at Terrance, a fellow mastiff, and his body type. The resemblance was eerie, even though Terrance ancestors were from Italy. It was like looking at himself if he had decided to take orders from the donut shop instead of the gym. The fur pattern was different, but to think that this could have been him. He wondered how Terrance could ever be content with himself.

Garth scanned the room again, wondering that about everyone else, too.

With the introductions out of the way, the gym coaches shuffled and traded papers back and forth. A few of these papers came Garth's way. They detailed the Basketball unit, football unit, soccer unit, badminton unit, and so forth. It looked like they were trying to decide which units to do first.

Garth sighed, thinking he would rather use a basketball to illustrate a distant star and how to calculate its mass by how much background light was bent around it. But he swallowed the depression and was about to recommend the option of basketball or tennis first, to give students a variety in choice, but nobody was even looking at the papers.

Garth stayed quiet, listened to the others. Conversation degenerated into complaining about the pups on their various teams and how poorly they performed last year on the soccer team, or the tennis team, or the gymnastics team. Jeremy's soccer team made it to state level in the competition, but that was it.

Some of the pups were part of both sports, and when two coaches could compare notes, they lamented they would have to work with these pups again. School policy meant they couldn't be cut from a team, so they were stuck with whoever they were stuck with.

After twenty minutes listening to three parallel conversations complaining about this pup and that one, Garth picked up some papers and spoke up.

"So are we here to figure out which units to do first?"

Sasha heard him and turned her muzzle his way. The gossip did not stop, and the multiple conversations between the different coaches were impenetrable. She too, rested her head in her paw and pretended to be part of the gossip in the room.

Garth leaned back in his chair and tried to listen, but it had all blended into white noise punctuated by laughter. He occupied his time by sorting them into the order he cared about. Basketball and football went at the end of the school year, soccer towards the middle, and weight training towards the front. He looked up from the papers, and the coaches were still rambling on about the pups over the previous years.

After an hour, Terrance called a break, and the group dispersed out the door, except for Garth and Sasha. She sat opposite the mastiff, and when everyone was out of the room, she smiled.

"Welcome to Montgomery High."

"Is this how we usually do things?"

Sasha nodded. "I've been here for three years. I gave up trying to get them to do anything."

"Is that both here and in class?"

"Vern is coaching tennis, and he teaches trig. You know what his major is? Music. Joey teaches physics and earth science, and he majored in electrical engineering. Terrance teaches economics, and he majored in anthropology. So what about you?"

"Physics."

She smiled again, nodded. "You're in good company here. I was lucky. I am a math major and I actually get to teach it, as much as you can call it teaching."

"So how do the rest of them survive?"

"We have class outlines, and we just follow them. Teach from the book. Every day we basically read the book to the students, make them take notes, give them tests every once in a while, and that's the course."

"Damn."

"They're probably going to stick you with social studies."

"I don't know social studies."

"They'll give you an outline, too, and a book. Just teach the textbook. It's what we have to do. It's actually required."

"Wait. Is this a coach's meeting, or—"

"Nope," Sasha said, smiling. "It's a teacher's meeting. There are two teams of four teachers per grade, and we basically do everything. Almost everyone has to coach something on the side. Sometimes we do the electives, too."

"So this is it? This is who is teaching our pups?"

Sasha nodded.

"This is extortion," Garth said. "They're making us do the work of two and three teachers but only paying us for one. How did the union approve this?"

"Budget cuts forced the teacher's union to agree. It happened years ago, long before I got here."

"Oh my God."

"We all feel your pain, Garth. I should be out there looking for consumer trends, tracking waste and extrapolating weather patterns. Instead, I'm reading a textbook to a bunch of high school pups and pretending to teach swimming. All the school cares about is the team you coach and how well you do in the regional and state competitions. That's what I have to do after school. By the time I get home, I might have time to eat and get five hours of sleep."

"Will I have to coach?"

"Maybe the school is looking to compete in the powerlifting circuits or something. I'm sure they hired you for just that reason. You look qualified for it."

Garth smiled, leaned back in his chair and sighed. "I'd rather be calculating trajectories to send people to Mars. I've been looking for a job for two years. Started with all the engineering posts, but nobody was hiring. Not even the military. Then I went for teaching positions at universities. Then I went down to high schools. This is the best job I could get."

"Two years. I believe it. I've been putting in applications for six. Nothing. So here I stay, coaching pups on the swim team. I'm one of six coaches on that alone. There are eight teachers managing the football teams, four for the tennis teams, and four for volleyball. It's gotten ridiculous, but it's not so bad once you accept that you're here to coach a sport, not teach a class. That's all this school cares about."

"Thanks for the warning." Garth looked down at the papers. "So when are we going to decide what to do this semester?"

"Maybe never, Terrance is supposed to be our team lead, but we're all coaches here. Nobody takes any of this seriously. It doesn't really matter in the end."

She turned her muzzle away, stared off into space. Garth flipped through the papers, made sure they were sorted in his order of preference. Five minutes later, the group began trickling back in, and the gossip resumed. Garth endured another twenty minutes of it.

He stared at the paper for the weightlifting unit. It seemed straightforward enough: demonstrate proper leg technique and various exercises designed to work the legs, demonstrate arm technique and five exercises. Very basic stuff, but pups needed to learn it sometime.

The mastiff looked up at Terrance. He growled, hating the smell of these "teachers," and hating that the last decade of his life had led him to this. He looked down at the papers, figuring since he was here he may as well do something he enjoyed.

Garth waited for a quiet spot in the student gossip and shouted. "Well, if there are no objections, I think these should be our first options."

He slid three papers to the center of the table for the weightlifting unit, the tennis unit, and the soccer unit. Everyone glared at him, as if the sentence he spoke had been made entirely of curse words. Garth did not care at all.

"Any thoughts?"

The other coaches looked at one another. Nobody spoke.

"Great," Garth said, and took the papers back.

"That reminds me," Terrance said. "Lilith wanted me to tell you to report to her after this meeting. I think she wants to assign you a class."

"Lilith?"

"Personnel Director, she hired you."

Garth glanced at Sasha. She smiled and nodded. Garth sighed. "Oh, that's her name. Sure, I'll see her."

Gossip resumed. Garth waited ten minutes, until the time slot for the meeting had elapsed, rose from his chair and walked out of the room. He breathed easier when he was out of there. He passed several more offices on the way to the office and stopped at the door labeled Personnel Department. He just now noticed the name on the door: Lilith Dover.

Garth turned the corner, tapped on the door. The poodle looked up from her desk. Her eyes brightened when she saw Garth.

"Mister Hood, I'm glad you're here." She picked up a folder on her desk. "As part of your employment here, I'm asked to inform you that you will be teaching our government course. It's for seniors only."

Garth walked in, took the folder from her and flipped though the papers inside. It was a course outline for Government Studies.

"Are you sure?" Garth said. "My major is in physics. Aren't there any openings in the science department?"

"Not at this time, Mister Hood. Also, if you keep going through the packet, you'll discover a proposal."

Garth flipped to the last page and skimmed it. He didn't need to read the whole thing. This one piece of paper was the whole reason he was hired, just as Sasha said. He caught several keywords: competition, wrestling team, and weightlifting.

He lowered the paper and met Ms. Dover's eyes. "They want me to get the wrestling team into weightlifting?"

"And the football team, too. You are definitely qualified, Mister Hood."

"I'm qualified to send people to the moon or mars."

"If K through twelve schools had space programs, I would have hired you for that in a heartbeat. But as it is, the school is looking to compete with the other teams in the state. All of the successful schools have integrated weight training into their student's routines. We are one of the last to do so."

Garth sighed, skimmed the paper again, and caught more keywords: collaborate, coaches, wrestling team, and football.

"Aren't there rules against this?" said the mastiff. "These are pups."

"Performance of the athletic department is a huge source of funding. We need to compete."

"Funding? This is high school."

"College teams recruit from our ranks, Mister Hood. We receive compensation from the sponsors when our numbers are good, and we need it, since the state decreased our operating budget eight years ago."

"And what about education? Science, reading, music? Does any of that matter these days?"

"Maybe when you and I went to school, but these days we have to follow the funding. Another chunk of our funding is also tied to test scores, and you would do well to make sure all of your students pass the tests. They're included in the course book. I am sure you can handle government studies, Mister Hood."

She smiled at him. It was not a professional smile.

Garth backed away from the desk. "All right, I'll work something out. Where do I get my supplies for the course?"

"Room two-oh-six, the educator's edition is in the desk."

"Thanks."

Garth backed all the way out.

"Oh, and by the way, Mister Hood. Everything I just told you is confidential."

Garth paused, head peeking around the door. "What was?"

"It was in your employment agreement. Issues relating to school budget and funding and operations are not to be discussed with the students, their families, or openly among other members of the faculty. Please treat it as protected information, Mister Hood."

Garth's muzzle was half open, trying to speak. He blinked twice, "Since when is stuff like that confidential?"

"Since the board decided it was best to keep it so."

"And when was that?"

"Eight years ago."

"Right. Sure."

He slinked away and walked down the hall, passing all the different offices. Richard Croshaw, Vice Principal. The counselor office. Garth paused by the door. There was only one Guidance Counselor's office. Garth remembered there was one for each grade when he was in high school, and he was certain his father told him there used to be two for each grade before that.

Garth shook his head, walked past the rest of the offices. He stopped at the door of the teacher's meeting he had left. The coaches were still in there, now laughing at one student on the baseball team who couldn't catch or bat, but still joined the team year after year.

He continued walking. In the adjacent room was another group of teachers. Past them, in another meeting room, was another. Each room was full of coffee cups, donut boxes, vending machine wrappers, soda cans and crumpled bags and French fry cartons. Garth recognized the Golden Halo logo on them. He hadn't eaten at that fast food place since he was in grade school, and it smelled as greasy and salty as he remembered.

He left the offices and walked down the empty halls. He growled to himself, clenched his fist, making his forearms stretch the sleeves of his shirt. A decade of school, and now his job was to get pups into weightlifting while pretending to teach government. He wondered how a dog who hadn't voted in years was supposed to educate the pups on the value of voting. Now he had less than a week to prepare two courses plus figure out how he was going to get the football and wrestling teams on weights, without betraying how the school system was playing puppetmaster with the students so it could secure more funding.

He growled louder when he realized his years of education had nothing to do with this job, only his dedication to the gym. He had no official qualifications for the task. He merely *looked* qualified to get the pups started on lifting weights. Garth bared his teeth and the fur on his back stood up as he thought about it. If he had known that was all he had to do to get a job, he wouldn't have bothered with university, and avoided the crippling debt that hung from his ballsack like a superhero's greatest weakness.

He wandered the lonely halls for a good ten minutes, passing janitors cleaning the floors and restrooms. Contractors were everywhere inspecting the sprinkler systems, fire extinguishers, pull stations, electrical systems, and various other things prior to the beginning of the school year. Some glanced at the large, growling mastiff passing by. Everyone stayed out of his way.

Finally, Garth arrived at the school's gymnasium. The bleachers were retracted, so the gymnasium looked huge. It had a drop ceiling, with the pipes and other fixtures hidden. He'd never seen that before; most schools were too cheap to put a drop ceiling above the gym so the balls wouldn't get stuck up there. At four basketball courts wide and three stories high, it was definitely where the school had spent the most money, and this didn't even include the pool.

Through one door off to the side, Garth saw dumbbell racks and exercise equipment. He walked across the shellacked floor painted with basketball court lines and stood in the single doorway.

Four benches lined the walls to his left and right. Against the far wall, in front of the two windows looking out on the courtyard, two squat racks stood side by side, and behind them were racks for leg-raises, chin-ups and calf-raises. Multi-purpose machines for the upper body and lower body groups were in the center, spaced far enough apart so nothing was in danger of colliding. A dumbbell rack ran along the wall with the door, stocked with weights ascending from 5 to 120. A few generic benches for free-weight moves were close by. It was a bit small, but there was plenty of room for everyone to have a routine and not bump into each other. No smell, no dirt, no tears on any of the seats or backrests.

Garth's face lifted and his tail wagged a little. His new job was to beef up the school's athletes to be more competitive, and he couldn't have asked for a better place to do it.

Chapter 3

The first bell rang. Garth stood stiff as a surfboard as the students began to arrive. This would be a freshman group, and all of a sudden Garth felt like an adult. Though he was in the small crowd of gym coaches, he felt alone and out of his element.

Garth wore a loose shirt, and gym shorts that hung down to mid-thigh. He would rather have covered up entirely, but this was gym and there was no other way. He also held a clipboard under one arm, and a whistle hung from his neck and rested between his pecs. He hoped he would never have to use it.

In five minutes, the second bell rang, and the students began filing in from the locker room, wearing shorts and loose shirts and ready to be physical this early in the morning.

The students gathered where the gym coaches were and Garth pretended to be occupied by something on his clipboard. He glanced up at the students from time to time. All of them were canine, and they were staring at him. Most looked intimidated, but a few seemed amazed. He caught whispers like "what's he doing here?" and "damn, who is that?" From any other crowd, Garth would have enjoyed the attention, but these were pups, so it felt awkward.

Terrance, the fat mastiff coach of basketball and economics, stepped out of the crowd of teachers and blew his whistle.

"Welcome to Montgomery High everyone! I'm Coach Terrance and we're going to start off with a couple unit choices. Everyone gets a choice of what to take, and this month we have either tennis, soccer or weight room. Coach Hood—" he gestured to Garth—"is gonna be doing the weight room unit. He's new this year so go easy on him."

Garth huffed. *Great, tell them I'm new and don't know what I'm doing.*

The students stared at him. Adults were discreet about it, but these pups were not.

With the brief introductions out of the way, Terrance lined the students up on the sideline. Garth stood in one spot in front of them. Four coaches stood in another spot a few feet away, then the other four stood in the other spot.

"Everyone who wants to do weights, line up in front of Garth," Terrance announced. He walked in a straight line to the next group. "Tennis is here." He stopped just after the last group and turned around. "Soccer is here."

The pups broke off the line and migrated to one of the three spots. Now Garth had a use for the clipboard. He clicked the pen, walked down the line, and got everyone's name. He had fourteen students in this period, which was probably all the weight room could handle.

He led the pups to the weight room, told them to take a seat anywhere. He gathered the papers from the unit outline that had been in the packet. Garth had looked it over and laughed. The outline was explicit in its instructions to use the included papers to illustrate proper technique. It outright warned instructors not to touch the weights themselves. Garth concluded the committee that wrote these guidelines possessed the collective intelligence of a neutrino, and decided to take the students through real demonstration, real hands-on training. The papers on the different muscle groups and all the exercises that worked them were useful though, and Garth passed those papers out.

"All right," Garth said. "My name is Mister Hood. I'll be doing the weight unit for the next three weeks. Those papers I gave you are just for reference. I'm going to take everyone through a basic chest and arm workout routine today, show you the machines, the weights, how to use them properly and how to keep yourself from getting injured. Let's start with the bench press. Everyone gather here, and make sure you can see."

He walked aside and stood by a bench. The students, one or two cats but mostly a mix of canine breeds and fur types, floppy ears and pointy ears, males and females, stood up and filtered between the equipment to the bench against the wall with the window.

On the advice of his fellow coaches, he did not demonstrate himself so he wouldn't be tired by the end of the day.

"I need a volunteer to demonstrate bench. Anyone want to show us how it's done?"

After half a beat of silence, a retriever raised his paw.

"Yes, what's your name?"

The retriever pushed past a couple dogs and now stood at the bench with Garth. "Tyler."

"Nice to meet you. You ever bench before?"

"A couple times."

"Well, I'll show you how to do it right."

Tyler seemed eager to be shown, and he stood opposite Garth as he explained how to start off with the bench press. Tyler lay down on it, Garth showed proper position of the bar, proper position of the hands. Tyler benched eighty pounds with some strain, which was good. As he benched, Garth guided his motions in the right direction, narrated why the hands had to be here, why the bar was positioned here, and most importantly, to never, ever, ever arch the back.

With the bench press out of the way, Garth moved the group to a couple different machines that did the same thing. Tyler demonstrated those, Garth narrated a bit, and then he moved on to arms. Tyler demonstrated for Garth as he narrated again. Garth made sure to tell him when he was doing it right, or in good form, or when his pacing was good so he wouldn't be intimidated or feel like Garth thought less of him.

They covered preacher curls, dumbbells, and barbell curls. He showed them proper posture, alignment of the back, position of the spine and shoulders. Garth hoped he was scaring the pups into keeping proper form and not taking chances.

Tyler set the dumbbells back on the rack.

"That's the basics," Garth said.

All through the period Garth had been reading the expression of the pups' faces, watching their body postures. They were intimidated, and that meant they were probably not paying attention.

Garth pulled out his cell phone, which he was not supposed to have with him, and showed Tyler a picture of himself when he was in the ninth grade when he was as small as the littlest dog in the room.

Tyler's face brightened and he laughed. Garth held his phone up to the other students, and their reactions ranged from arms-folded indifference, to ear-perking disbelief.

"Don't think it can't pay off," Garth said to everyone as he slipped his phone back in his pocket. "And you don't even have to go as far as I have! Even doing it casually, you'll see a difference. Now, for the rest of the period, I want you all to work the arms and chest. Don't try to do too much weight, don't hurt yourself. Stick with the basics. If you have any questions, just ask."

The students dispersed around the weight room. It was easy to tell who came here because they wanted to work out, and who came here because they thought they could get away with standing around talking the whole time. A group of teenage females sat on a bench in the corner, talking, pulling out notebooks and doing homework that should have been done yesterday.

Garth was about to tell them this wasn't a study hall, but Tyler and two other dogs approached him.

"Coach Hood?" said a young pit bull standing next to Tyler. "We're on the football team. We were told to see you."

Garth blinked. It was the first time anyone had called him that. Thinking it was bizarre, but to hear it from someone else was uncomfortable.

"First, please don't call me coach. Mister Hood will be fine."

The pups looked confused. Garth didn't give them a chance to think about it. He led them out of the weight room, through the gymnasium and into the locker rooms, where the coaches' offices were. His office was a tiny room with a desk pushed flush against the wall opposite the door, just barely large enough for himself and a couple other people to stand. He had a feeling it was originally for the janitor.

Garth really wanted to keep an eye on the other pups to make sure they didn't hurt themselves, but he remembered why he was hired, and spent the remainder of the period in his tiny office asking the pups questions, figuring out what a good routine would be for them, as well as assigning them a diet.

Those pups left his office with a bounce to their step. Garth sat back in his chair and smiled. Would they have accepted a workout routine and diet plan from someone who obviously didn't have either? The workouts wouldn't begin until next week and Garth would be in the weight room the whole time. He considered actually working out with them. Perhaps seeing him go through his routine would give them a little taste of jealousy and inspire them to push themselves harder.

The bell rang, first period dismissed and Garth gathered with the other coaches in the gymnasium. At the next bell, Garth took attendance, and the students were divided into the units.

Second period was a repeat of the first. Garth was afraid of what would happen if there was no volunteer to demonstrate the moves, but this period had a volunteer, too, and Garth used him so show everyone chest and arms.

After the demonstration, the football and wrestling pups cornered him and Garth took them aside and gave them a workout and diet program. Many of them, to his surprise, did not know the first thing about exercise or proper diet, and to these pups he promised more thorough instruction beginning next week after school.

The next two periods went just the same, and he showed the pictures of himself on his phone more than he expected. He always kept those old pictures of him on it because nobody believed he used to be "ordinary," and it helped break past the intimidation Garth had to deal with when meeting anybody for the first time. Bringing himself down to their level reassured him he was a person, just like they were. By the time class dismissed, he felt more like he was making new friends than taking his place as a teacher.

Fifth period hit, and it was time to change clothes and become a government teacher. He noticed most of the other coaches didn't bother to change clothes when they transitioned from coach to teacher, but Gath did so anyway. Long shorts and a shirt showed just enough to let the pups know he practiced what he preached, but in the classroom it would not help him at all.

So he walked into fifth period Government Studies well before the bell rang and sat behind his new desk. The classroom was arranged so the doorway was parallel with the teacher's desk, and all the students were facing the wall with the door. When Garth was a student, he disliked classrooms set up this way, as students passing by in the hall peeked in and distracted him. Now that he was the teacher, it worked in his favor. He used the time now to skim over the lesson he had to give today.

He had reviewed the class outline during his time leading up to the first day of school. He expected to be crushed under the weight of planning lessons and lectures and assignments, but to his surprise he found all of that was done for him.

The outline had everything, from quizzes to hand out, to questions to ask the students to keep them paying attention, to tests at the end of every section. Garth even skimmed the final exam. It was all here, premade, the entire course. Even the lectures he was supposed to give in class were the book itself. The textbook was written like a class lecture, and the outline instructed him to "lecture the text, using the additional notes in the margin to elaborate on certain points."

These "additional notes" were written in the margin of the educator's edition, and the students didn't see them. Some of the quiz questions asked specifically about the information in those notes, to make sure the students were paying attention.

Garth may have had a doctorate, but he was not trained to teach, so he was relieved he didn't have to go through all the work of making a brand new class in less than a week. He really could just jump right into this.

The students arrived. Garth passed out the books, opened to the first lesson and began paraphrasing the entire chapter. It began with a history of government, how it was believed government began, and the cruel, early forms of it that were not very fair, but kept the population orderly so civilization could survive. He made sure to include the "additional notes" in his lecture.

When he was done, Garth assigned the quiz at the end of the chapter, passed out the multiple choice forms, and let the pups work on the assignment for the remainder of class. Garth sat behind his desk and settled in. Several dogs and one feline rose from their desks and walked up to him.

"Coach Hood?"

"Not coach. I'm Mister Hood."

Again the pups were confused.

"Football team?" Garth said.

They nodded. Garth asked the usual questions and told them to meet up with him after school for more formal instruction. They looked him over, eager to hear what he had to say—eager to receive the workout program. Garth smiled as they took their seats. By the end of the period, all the students had turned in their papers, the bell rang, and the students rushed to their next class. Garth took a few deep breaths, rinsed his mind and prepared to do it all over for his second period of government studies.

The students took their seats. One doberman in the back caught his eye because he was staring at Garth harder than any of the others. Most of the pups looked and smelled intimidated when meeting Garth for the first time, but the doberman had a different look about him. The dobie was wearing a shirt that was exactly his size, showing off his lithe torso just as much as a jock would wear a tight shirt to show off his bulk. He was thin, but not lanky or disgusting. Not just a thin dog, but toned. Garth had never seen a pup deliberately show that off before. He easily stood out in a group for this alone, and unlike everyone else, he didn't turn his head when Garth looked at him directly.

Garth rose from his desk. "Hello, everyone. I'm Mister Hood, your Government Studies teacher."

He passed out the books and began his lecture with the opening chapter of government's early years. The doberman in the back was actually paying attention. There was an eagerness to his eyes that seemed too adult to be in high school.

Garth paused to ask one of the suggested questions. "Anyone know what the earliest record of government is?"

The dobie raised his hand.

"Yes, what's your name again?"

"Evan Silvers. Uh, they told me to talk to you. I'm on the wrestling team."

Garth couldn't help but laugh a little. "*You're* on the wrestling team?"

The class giggled with Garth, but he didn't get the feeling they were laughing at Evan. The dobie nodded, smiling.

"Do you have gym next period?"

He nodded.

"See me then. I'll get you hooked up."

The pup smiled and paid attention again as Garth resumed the lecture.

The other students had that body posture that said, *I'd rather be on my phone texting.* Garth was pretty sure they were writing text messages in their minds right now, anticipating responses and coming up with what they would say afterwards.

Not Evan. He was listening, and he never took his eyes off Garth. At first Garth was thrilled someone at least acted like they cared about the course,

but after half an hour, that look became unnerving. Evan was too attentive. Too interested.

Garth was glad when the lecture was over and he let the class work alone. It meant he got to sit behind the desk and pretend to do things on the computer. Several times Garth looked up and caught Evan staring at him. The first few times, Evan turned his muzzle down and pretended to be absorbed in the quiz. The last time, the dobie did not look away. He held Garth's eyes.

The mastiff's first reaction was to wave at him, but he was a teacher now, so he tapped his finger on his desk, hoping he was gesturing to get back to work. The dobie pup smiled, his ears forward and alert, and resumed the assignment. As the pups finished, they got louder and louder until the bell rang.

Garth had one more gym class this day, so he had to change out of teacher clothes and back into his gym clothes. Garth could understand why so many coaches didn't bother to change, as this would become tiresome quickly, but Garth was determined to do his best even when it was inconvenient.

Last period was gym class. The students lined up and separated the weight-room pups from the tennis and soccer pups. Evan was in class, and he was first in line for the weightlifting unit.

As usual, Garth asked for a volunteer for demonstrations. The dobie stepped forward, sat down on the bench and picked up a modest weight for the arm curls. He did a few sloppy curls, and Garth stopped him, held his own arm next to Evan's and showed proper technique. Wrist straight, elbow straight, back straight.

Evan imitated him, staring at Garth's arm. His form instantly improved. With that done, he led the group to the bench and Evan demonstrated. The dobie seemed to know how to bench press, but Garth spotted him and adjusted the bar to the correct position.

When the instruction was over, half the students sat around and did homework or talked or played on their phones. The other half hit the weights. Again, Garth wanted to whip them all into shape, but the eight wrestling and football players needed his attention. Garth took them to his office and figured out a good workout program to start with.

The dobie stood against the wall the whole time, letting everyone else go before him. Finally, the other dogs left the room, and it was just the two of them. Garth noticed the dobie's crotch. It was sticking out obscenely far. He pretended not to notice.

"Well Evan, seems you're the only one in class today who actually wanted to get his paws on the weights."

Evan smiled, half looking away. "Well, I've kinda wanted to for a while. Always wanted to get big."

Garth smiled. "Don't think it can't happen." He reached for his phone, pulled up the usual picture of himself as a sophomore. Not as thin as the dobie, but thin enough that nobody would ever have guessed his future. He handed the phone to Evan.

Evan stared at it for a moment. "That's you?"

Garth smiled, turned back to his desk. "As a freshman. Anything is possible. So you're on the wrestling team? First year on it?"

"Actually no, I've been on it since my freshman year."

"How's it goin' for you?"

"Okay, I guess. I'm quick and flexible and can take a pounding."

"Well, now the school wants you to put some meat on those bones." Garth took out pencil and paper. Every time he did this he felt like he was writing a prescription. "Here's a workout routine and diet plan. It's a good place to start. If you want to stay on the wrestling team, you'll need to log workouts twice a week, report to the nurse once of a month for a physical. I'm working with the other coaches on a schedule."

He paused, looked up at the pup. The dobie was swiping through his pictures.

"Give me that!"

Evan looked up from the phone, smiled and handed it back. Garth took it, turned the phone back around and glanced at the screen. Evan had stopped on a picture Garth took of himself at the beach over the summer from a low angle, making his pecs look like mountains. He kept his fur so finely trimmed every nook and cranny on his upper body was visible.

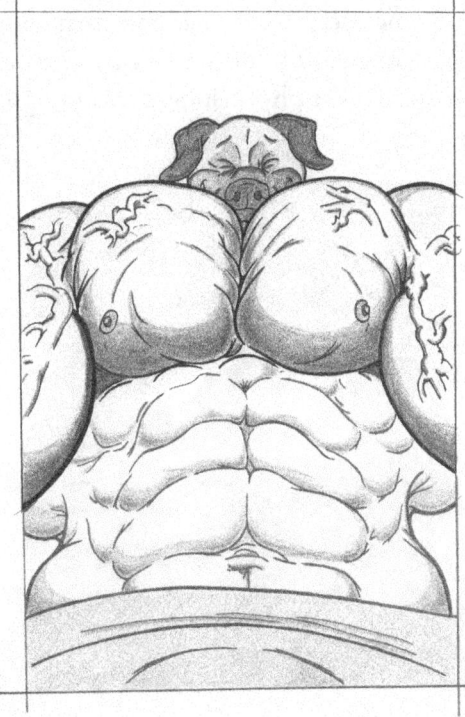

Evan was still smiling, and that look... The same look he had been giving Garth in class. Here it was again.

Garth set the phone down with one paw and handed the paper to him with the other. "Workouts start next week Evan, as well as practice. I guess they started signups for all the extracurricular activities before school even began. Never heard of that before, but seems everything is filled up and ready to go. Who's your coach?"

"Coach Bob."

"You mean Coach Campbell?"

"Nobody calls him that. He insists on Bob."

"All right, that's fine then. And I insist you don't call me coach at all. I am Mister Hood."

Evan finally took the paper, turned halfway around and walked to the door. He turned back again, still giving Garth that look. Garth returned the stare. This time he didn't keep up the pretense of being a teacher. He held the pup's stare for as long as it took, hoping he was giving Evan the same look, whatever it was.

Evan raised his upstage arm, made a muscle, twitched his ears, nodded to his arm and then to Garth's, smiled and whistled. He turned around and trotted back to the gymnasium.

The physicist held the stare to the empty doorway.

Chapter 4

Garth always wondered what a teacher's lounge looked like. He had one period to himself for lunch, just as the students did, but yesterday was such a rush to be places and figure out what he was doing that he didn't even have time to peek inside. Today he made it a point to come here.

It wasn't like he saw on TV shows at all. It was a break room like any other, with a few chairs and tables. No fancy furniture, just a TV on a stand in the corner. He was disappointed, but with the way things were going since he graduated, he wasn't surprised anymore.

Garth inspected the vending machines, found nothing of value and sat down for his usual meal. His priority was to work his diet and supplement into his new schedule, and he had a shaker bottle of protein-infused water and a large plate of fish. People teased him for that all the time in university, how only felines liked fish, but Garth never liked the taste of most of the red meats canines were supposed to favor because it was always blended with soy and corn to make it cheaper.

He was the only teacher in here right now, which he thought was odd. He was hoping to meet more of the other teachers, especially the science teachers. He hoped to ask if they needed help in some way.

Minutes later, a familiar scent walked through the door, her fur damp and smelling of chlorine.

"Sasha!" Garth said.

"Coach Hood, good to see you."

Garth shuddered. "Please don't call me coach. I'm a damn physicist."

Sasha smiled, walked over to his table and leaned on it. "I know. I've heard some pups talk about a coach who doesn't like to be called coach. They're laughing at you, you know?"

"If they knew their gym teacher had a PhD in physics, they wouldn't."

Still smiling, Sasha sat down, facing Garth. "How's it going trying to get the pups into weights?"

"I think I've met everyone by now. Got them started on paper, but the workouts won't start until next week. Then I guess my job will be to make sure they stick to it. I plan to watch them close, make sure they don't hurt themselves."

"Told you they hired you for a reason."

Garth closed his eyes, shook his head. "Yeah, they hired me for my body, not my mind."

"Welcome to a female's world."

Garth smiled, took a swig from the bottle and looked at her. "So how often do you actually get in the water?"

"Almost never."

"It's that annoying?"

"I hate chlorine. I may be a pool instructor, but that's all I have to do, instruct. That doesn't mean I have to get in."

"What about the pups who can't swim? What do they get?"

"That's for one of the other coaches to deal with."

"Do they teach them to swim?"

"That would require getting in the water."

"Oh. Sorry, I thought maybe school would consider teaching the pups something."

"Garth, I would teach every one of those children how to swim if the school gave me the time I needed. But I have almost two hundred pups. I can't teach everyone. So I give them some basic lessons, give a written test, and that's the course. If they can swim, I give them diving exercises, relay races, object retrieval, things like that. The school didn't build the pool to teach kids to swim. They built it to compete with other swim teams. The more prestigious we are, the more funding we get. All I can do is try not to smell too much like pool water by the time I have to teach math."

"Yeah, I get ya. I'm probably going to spend the whole day watching the pups exercise. At least I don't have to grade papers."

"It's not really a good thing."

"Seems good to me, I gave a quiz at the end of my government classes yesterday. Took the papers to the machine, two minutes later I had results. Didn't have to waste an hour grading them."

Sasha shook her head. "Everything is multiple choice, five choices maximum. Computer grades everything for you in seconds. You'd think it would be a relief, but faculty discourages us from doing anything that can't be graded by computer now. You know what that means?"

"How is a bad thing? Would you want to spend hours every day grading papers by hand? That's work I'm happy to avoid."

"You're a physicist. Think about Newton's first law. For every advance in technology, there's a push back on us. All it does is give the brass an excuse to downsize us and push more work on the survivors."

"Oh."

"Even my math exams are multiple choice, Garth. Pups don't have to do the problems to pass. They just try all the answers in their calculators until something works. Even pups who don't pay attention can pass because they know how to take the tests. I'd rather give them something that makes them do the work. If that means having to spend hours being a teacher, that's fine by me. No more chlorine fur."

"Well, I could do that. It's my government class. I could make a project for them. Do something that would require some effort. Something big. A report, a presentation."

Sasha leaned on the table, sliding forward, head in her paws. "I hope you do, but it happens to everyone who comes here. They'll pack your schedule so full you won't have time to do anything outside the box."

"I'll find a way. As long as I'm here I should try to do a good job. Dad always told me to go above and beyond. Employers recognize that."

"Oh, they recognize it all right." Sasha stood up. "Just don't let yourself get fat and lazy. I'm going to the cafeteria for a bite to eat. See you later."

"Bye."

The shepherd/collie plunked some coins into the snack machine, took the package that fell, and walked out the door. Garth ate alone for the rest of his period. Nobody else came to the lounge, and the emptiness of the room was unnerving. He looked around at the various posters lining the walls, one for every subject in school.

The chemistry poster showed a child's mind represented by a beaker full of ideas waiting to burst out. The caption read: *Be the catalyst.*

An English poster showed an archetypical teacher standing between a young puppy and the word FUTURE. *You are the conjunction.*

A Home Economics poster with no caption showed more teacher archetypes showing student archetypes having a lot of fun cooking, doing laundry and planning careers.

One poster caught his eye. It was simply an image of the moon. The caption read *Carpe Lunam.*

Garth half-smiled. It was just corny enough to be brilliant.

"I'm trying," he said to the poster.

There was plenty of time for his mind to wander to all the places he would rather be.

His Government classes were as boring for him as they must have been for the pups. The outline told him to read the very chapter he had assigned them to read last night, most of whom had read it in class. This chapter was about ancient governments around the world, how they differed based on location, and how geography and culture shaped them. It was merely an overview of ancient cultures from the point of view of their government, with supplemental material from the additional notes in the margins.

He incorporated the extra notes into his reading, asked the students questions when those notes prompted him to do so. The notes listed possible responses to these questions and suggested responses he should give, but there was no discussion, no dialogue. The students would rather be texting.

When he had reached the end, there was still half an hour left of class, so Garth assigned the next chapter as homework and gave the students the other half of the period to work on their homework in class. None of this was his decision. It was written in the outline.

Garth projected this into the near future and saw how boring and routine this would become, both for himself and the students. He took out a piece of paper and began jotting down ideas for things he could make the students do that would force them to think outside a multiple choice exam. Reports he could assign, research papers, current event studies. There were so many possibilities, and all it would take was a little time.

Next period, Garth found it difficult to maintain his composure with Evan staring at him the whole time. The dobie was the only one paying attention while Garth read the book, looking up at the students only to say something from the notes on the margin. In a room full of slouching pups resisting the urge to pull out their cell phones and text someone in another class, Evan looked like a space alien.

Garth faked his way through the rest of the course, then sat at his desk and jotted down more ideas for something he could do to make this class relevant and interesting. A nonfiction book report, a comparison/contrast of the systems of two different nations.

A moment later, Garth smelled Doberman nearby.

"Mister Hood?"

Garth looked up and met Evan Silvers' eyes.

"You okay? You look pretty rough."

Garth was speechless for a second. A student treating him like an actual person? This pup must have been from outer space.

"I'm fine, Evan. First week of school is always tough."

Evan smiled. Now Garth recognized it. It was the same, unprofessional smile Ms. Dover gave him the other day.

"You figured out how this school works yet?" Evan said in a low voice.

Garth held his breath for a moment. Evan continued.

"Did they tell you what happened to the last coach who did this class?"

"Did you know him?" Garth said.

"Coach Bergeaud. He was one of the wrestling coaches. I heard from one of the seniors he basically told the pups in Government the class was a joke, that he didn't know anything about government, and it's a study hall now. It lasted a month, then someone found out and he got fired. They replaced him with someone else who just read from the book."

"Well..." Garth began. He leaned forward in his chair, too late realizing the shirt pulled tight against his chest muscles. "He was right."

The dobie's gaze definitely went lower than Garth's eyes. Then he looked up again. "All the pups in my class figured it out. It's how the whole school is. Once we figured out the teachers didn't know anything, we stopped working, and we still pass."

Garth smiled. "Let's just say things are a lot different from when I was your age."

Garth couldn't believe he had said it. It was the ultimate old dog expression, like 'when I was your age' or 'back in my day'. It finally happened, and he didn't feel a day over twenty. "But I won't let that happen," he continued. "I'm probably gonna give out a report or something in the future. Something that's not multiple choice."

"Coach Bergeaud tried that. Told the pups to read and do an analysis of ten news stories online. Everyone got perfect scores, even the people who did tabloid articles."

Garth laughed a little. "My standards are a little higher."

The answer seemed to satisfy the dobie. He smiled wider, eyes darting from Garth's chest, to his arms, to his stomach.

"Next period is legs?" he said.

Garth nodded. "Legs and back. Pay special attention to back safety. Do not screw up your back."

"I'm pretty flexible," he said, never wiping that grin from his face. He leaned closer. "I can suck myself."

Garth's eyes widened. If he met Evan any other place, he would have loved to continue this conversation, but he was a teacher now, and he had to draw a line somewhere.

"Take a seat, Evan. I'll see you next period."

Still smiling unprofessionally, Evan pushed away from the desk and walked to the back of the classroom. Garth jotted down more ideas for projects he could assign.

Next period, Garth did his final lesson on leg and back routines, and Evan was his volunteer again. Garth made sure his form was right, corrected him when he dipped too low on squats.

For the back exercises, Garth demonstrated those personally and made damn well sure the pups were paying attention. He showed them all the ways they could hurt their back, incorrect posture, arching, twisting, and so on, and how to avoid those ways.

For his final demonstration, Garth sat in the rowing machine and showed them proper posture and technique, where to keep the hands and how to tell if you were leaning too far forward or backwards.

Evan raised his hand. Garth called on him.

The dobie stood with his arms close to his body. He had a real puppy dog look on his face, and so did his scent, which stood out among the normal teenage scents in the room.

"So... How much can you row?"

Nobody laughed. Some of the other pups noticed that the twig had the guts to ask the question, and joined in.

"Yeah, coach, how much do you row?"

"Show us!"

"Come on!"

Garth smiled. Their eagerness to see what Garth could do was so refreshing after two periods of indifference in government studies.

"Don't call me coach, Evan. But since you had the courage to actually ask me, I'll show you where I am."

He leaned forward, removed the pin and placed it into the two-hundred and ten slot. He then rowed a few times, keeping his form even more perfect and uniform than he normally did. The pups collectively gasped and murmured. To them, it looked impossible for that much weight to move at all. He only did three reps, and then he let the weights settle gently and climbed out of the machine.

"I've been doing this for almost twenty years. Don't forget that, everyone," he shouted over the chatter. "You're young, you're just starting out, and I promise if you keep it up, you can be where I am. Not everyone can, but that's okay, you go as far as you like with it. Exercise is the important part, keeping the body active. The body was designed to be active, and if you keep it, it will stay healthy. Do it safely and you'll never have a problem. Now everyone start working out. Legs and back. Be extra careful with the back. Do not hurt yourselves. You hurt yourself, and I will hurt you for being stupid."

The pups had begun to disperse around the weight room while he talked. He noticed some of the girls in the corner standing around, talking to each other, or other males, curling a five pound weight in one hand. There was a group of them every period. Pups who didn't want to do anything, so they just picked a dumbbell and curled it the whole period.

"Ladies," Garth said. "You did that yesterday. Do something with lower body today."

They collectively glared at him, rolled their entire heads instead of just their eyes, and wandered over to the leg press, where they took turns doing one or two reps, laughing at how little they could do. Being able to lift or press as little as possible seemed to be a badge of honor among these groups.

Garth considered giving everyone a paper to fill out, with various workout moves, weight used, sets and reps, and making the unit a requirement to fill out the paper, tracking their progress.

Most of the other students were actually working out, and Garth wandered around, observing them as they did lower body workouts. He corrected forms, made sure the ones doing back moves were not about to mess up.

He saw one pit bull grab a twenty-pound plate, hold it to his chest and perform what looked like twisting good-mornings.

"Hey!" Garth shouted. "What did I tell you?! Do not twist when working the back!"

The student realized Garth was talking to him and held still, standing with the plate against his chest. Garth walked in front of him.

"What were you doing?!"

"Modified good-mornings, I saw it on the internet."

Garth sneered. "Don't do that again. Don't do anything you read on the internet that involves twisting or arching. Never, never, never twist or arch your back."

"Sure, Co— Mister Hood."

"Now let me see you do good-mornings properly."

The pit bull repeated the exercise without twisting. Garth watched him, counted his reps.

"That's better, much better. That's a good weight for you for now. When you can do that for ten reps easily, add five pounds. Use a barbell next time."

Garth yearned for the days when taking a ruler to a student's paw was acceptable. He turned around, observed the other students using the equipment. No other problems so far.

Evan was by himself at a squat rack, holding the bar and two five-pound weights on either end, looking like he was about to break. The dobie was dipping too far again. Garth growled and weaved between the various benches and machines and stood beside Evan.

"You don't have to sit down Evan. Thighs parallel to the floor is far enough."

"I'm used to going all the way down," he said as he stood up, looking at Garth, smiling. The motion pushed his crotch out.

Garth stared. Evan's crotch would enter the room before the pup did. He was sure it didn't do that when he demonstrated before.

Evan was looking at him. That smile was still on his face. "So how much do you squat?"

Garth only heard every other word.

"Mister Hood," Evan said.

Now Garth heard him. "Uh, probably three or four times what you weigh."

Evan's smile spread into a grin that showed his teeth. He squatted again, and when he rose, his crotch was even more obscene, sticking out farther than his muzzle.

"Evan. Period's almost up. Put the weights up and get changed into something less..."

Evan's smile became downright predatory as he stepped back, placed the barbell on the rack and undid the weights. Garth stood by the door, watching the students file from the gymnasium and then into the locker rooms. A paw smacked Garth's ass, and Evan trotted out of the weight room. He was the last to leave.

"Shit," Garth whispered.

Chapter 5

Garth turned the corner and stood in Ms. Dover's door. She was at her desk again, at seven in the morning, one hour before class began.

"You wanted to see me?"

"Yes, Mister Hood, have a seat please."

Garth stepped into the office and sat in the same chair in which he was interviewed for his job a couple weeks ago. Ms. Dover had turned around in her chair and was flipping through a drawer in a file cabinet against the wall.

"How are you this Friday morning?" she said.

"A bit overwhelmed by all the stuff I have to do, but so far so good."

"Glad to hear it, glad to hear it. I've heard good things about you, Garth. The pups are impressed by you."

"They respect me in the gym. Not so much the classroom. I think they will even more when their routines actually begin next week."

"And how have you been getting along with the other coaches?"

"Haven't seen much of them so far, but I've been working with Joey, Bob, and Paul and a few others. They've taken a look at the routines I've assigned their athletes and I think they approve. We have a schedule for practice and workouts beginning Monday. I plan to be in the weight room every day the students have practice to make sure they stick to their routines and don't hurt themselves."

Ms. Dover closed the metal drawer and turned around in her chair, holding a small stack of papers in front of her. "Did they seem resentful?"

"What do you mean?"

"I was a little concerned some of the other coaches would resent a stranger giving their students workout routines they themselves could easily have given out."

Garth smiled. "The students would never have taken them seriously."

Ms. Dover smiled and handed the papers to Garth. *Moderator Guidelines for Student Council* was the header. He skimmed the rest.

"Were you ever on Student Council, Mister Hood?"

"No. Why?"

"Meetings begin next week, and we lack a moderator. As the teacher of Government Studies, you would be perfect for the job."

"Perfect? I don't know anything about government."

"But you have a good deal of life experience under your belt, Mister Hood. That alone makes you more qualified than the students to help them through a democratic process."

"My life experience has been in university."

"Surely you have experience working with others and helping them to come to some agreement."

"A little."

"You can handle this. The students respect you. You'll have no trouble keeping them focused and civil."

"Why me? I have a full schedule, and now the school is asking me to do the jobs four people used to do. I'm only being paid for one of those jobs."

"Paid very well."

"Compared to the other jobs I applied for, no. Ms. Dover, my after school time will be packed making sure those athletes don't hurt themselves on the squat rack. I need to be there."

"Student Council meets once a week for two hours. You have time for that, don't you?"

Garth skimmed the papers she handed him and tried to keep his fur down.

"Ms. Dover, this is getting ridiculous. First the school wants me to teach Government Studies with less than a week to prepare, then I find out I'm supposed to get all the athletes started on a weightlifting program, and I don't have the qualifications for either. Now I'm in charge of Student Council, too."

"You've done very well in Government Studies, despite your misgivings."

"I'm reading the book to the pups."

"Your job will be to moderate and guide the Student Council for a couple hours on Wednesdays. That's not too much to ask, Mister Hood."

"Actually, it says right here—" Garth pulled one of the papers from the stack and showed it to Ms. Dover. "I will be in charge of putting issues before the group and ensuring the voted measures are passed to the appropriate people for action. That means I'm going to do all the legwork of the Student Council."

"It won't take very long, Mister Hood."

"Frankly, I don't believe that. Any other surprises you have for me? Any other jobs I'm going to do? No more surprises. Let's hear it. What else do you have planned for me?"

"That is all at this time."

"What about next week? Or next month? Is the school going to make me tutor some pups in advanced physics during my lunch?"

"Would you like to?"

"Give somebody else Government Studies and I can teach physics. I'll give these pups the best physics course they'll ever have."

"We already have a physics instructor."

"He's an electrical engineer, and he coaches the wrestling team. I'd hate to know what the pups are learning."

"Exactly what the textbook states."

"Why hire teachers? Why not replace us with online videos? That's already happening in some universities. Tuition costs are rising, and yet they're cutting back on the professors. You can't tell me the education value is rising."

"Universities are tied to funding just the same as we are. Everybody has to become more efficient and multitalented in order for the school to stay open. I have faith in you, Mister Hood. I know you can get this done."

"Faith? Don't give me faith. Give me time."

"I can give you some time, Garth."

Garth's ears perked up slightly. "What?"

Ms. Dover gave him an unprofessional smile again. "It is Friday, so perhaps we can continue this discussion later. Away from school."

Garth's ears lowered and the fur on the back of his neck rose. "Let's keep this professional, Ms. Dover."

She smiled wider, and then it became professional again. "Of course, Mister Hood. Let me know if you have any concerns."

"Right."

Garth stood up, folded the papers, walked out the door, turned the corner and bumped into Sasha Grace.

"Oop—" Garth mumbled, dodged and walked by her. "Sorry."

A moment later, Garth heard claw clicks on the floor catching up to him, and she walked beside him, matching his pace.

"Was that what I think it was?" Sasha said.

Garth growled. His fur was up.

"Was she seriously hitting on you?"

"It's my damn fault. Its how I got this job."

"What, 'cause she thinks you're hot?"

"I let her do it. I should've known it's the only reason she hired me."

Sasha giggled. "Maybe you should. Might be the only way to get a promotion around here."

"No! I have PhD, Sasha! I shouldn't have to suck up to bosses! I shouldn't have to coach high school gym! I shouldn't have to beg for a goddamned job! I shouldn't have to do this shit!"

"Garth."

He turned, and saw she had retreated into one of the classrooms. Garth followed her and closed the door behind her. They were in an English room. The marker board was full of sentence diagrams, with verbs written in red, nouns in black, adjectives in green and adverbs in yellow. It looked like graffiti to Garth's eyes.

"I'm in charge of Student Council now. I'm going to be the dog who makes sure their votes actually change things! When am I supposed to do that?"

"Garth, I get it. This place is shit. It really is."

Garth's fur was only halfway down. He sat in a student's chair, dropped the pack of papers on the desk and looked at the floor. "Is it only going to get worse?"

Sasha sat on the desk in front of Garth's. "Give them another week and they'll put something else on you. They made me mediator of Odyssey of the Mind."

"What's that?"

"National competition, a problem-solving contest basically. So between coaching the swim team and trying to show my students how to actually solve quadratic equations, I also have to sit behind a desk and listen to high-schoolers figure out how to work in a group to solve some contrived problem."

"Was it always like this?" Garth said, looking up at her. "Was there a time when teachers volunteered for this stuff?"

"I wouldn't know. But sometimes it is interesting, watching students come up with solutions. My job is to keep their ideas on budget, and also to keep the group from excluding ideas that might be useful. It's only for a few months out of the year, but it still cramps my schedule, especially when the swim team starts competing."

Garth growled. "Two years of job hunting. Ten years in school. Look at me. Why the hell did I bother? What was I hoping for?"

"Math and physics are pretty useless in the world of normal jobs, Garth." Sasha said, grinning.

"Follow my dream my ass. I wish someone had told me otherwise when I was in high school. No, they were just thrilled to load me with me debt."

"Education is a business now."

"That's the difference."

Sasha smiled. "Well, if you need to vent again, let me know. None of the others will talk about it. They've been here too long. I think they've convinced themselves this is how it's always been and how it should be."

"Thanks."

Sasha was still smiling down at him.

"You're not gonna hit on me, too, are you?"

Her smile spread just a little and her tail waved around. "You're not my type. Lilith Dover would have been until I realized..." She trailed off, gritted her teeth and growled.

"Yeah, I hear ya. Never cared for the ladies myself."

Sasha laughed, never breaking eye contact. "I knew it! I can always tell when I'm talking to another gay dog! They don't want something from me, they're not always dropping hints."

Garth nodded, tail twitching beside the chair. "I've heard that before."

"Better keep it to yourself. There's no law against it, but the school will fire you if they find out. Even if nobody complains, they will still fire you just in case."

"I figured." He looked at the clock. "Well, it's almost time. I've got some papers to give to my students. Better make sure everything is ready."

"Me too," she reached over, rested paw on his shoulder. "Hang in there, Garth. We're all on the same side." Sasha stood and walked to the door.

"You, too," Garth said. "Good luck staying out of the water."

"It's Friday," she said, holding the door. "It will take an act of God to get me in today."

Garth sat still for a moment longer. He wanted to quit, right now, before this place go to him. But he had loans maturing, rent to pay and food to buy. He had been living off his leftover student loan money since graduation, and it was running out. This was the only job he found in two years that paid something close to a living wage. Quitting was not an option. The mastiff got out of the chair and left the classroom.

Today he handed all his gym students the very papers he imagined the other day. He had crafted them up at home the night before, printed one copy, ran off a hundred more at the school's copier just before Ms. Dover called him to his office. At least now the students had some structure to the days in gym, and some of them actually put in some time on the weights.

Today was shoulders and triceps, and Garth used his usual volunteers to demonstrate the various exercises and equipment. They now had basic moves for the entire body. Garth still had to watch them. Even after his careful instruction, some of them still tried to do dumb things.

Two students shared a barbell and were trying to curl it together. Garth ran over and stopped them, reminding them this was not a place to play around. Had they been serious about exercise, Garth would have applauded the technique, but since they were only playing around, it had to stop.

Third period Garth walked around the corner, making it look like he had left the room, and listened. The students were talking about him.

"What's Coach Hood doing here?" he heard one of them say.

"Wonder how much he benches."

"His arms are bigger than my legs. And he's a high school gym coach?!"

"Wonder what he did to get like that."

"Roids?"

"Doesn't seem to."

Garth smiled. Boys gossiped as much as girls, just different topics. He leaned against the door and continued listening.

Then Government Studies came. Garth was there long before his class started, and he stood at the door while the students swarmed the halls. In the distance he saw Evan, flanked by a rottweiler and a coyote, both twice his size. Garth stared at them, puzzled. They looked like they were escorting him to his class, but they were also much too close to him for normal friends. He couldn't hear what they were talking about, but all three seemed to share the same smile. They turned a corner and walked into a classroom three doors down.

By now the bell rang, and Garth stepped inside his own classroom and stood in front of his desk, facing a full house of students. Garth had time yesterday to read the chapter they were covering today, so he gave a real lecture, incorporating the margin notes and asking questions at the right time. For the first time, he felt like a teacher, and got some actual participation from the students. Most were silent and disinterested, but a few seemed to be paying attention.

During the second period of government, even Evan seemed distant. Garth hoped the pup realized he had crossed a line, thought about how stupid he had been, and would now back off.

During his final weight room period, Garth handed out the last of the workout charts and used Evan to demonstrate triceps and shoulders. Evan was in good form today, and needed little correction.

Garth let the students begin. The paper had suggestions for which days to work which muscle groups, and walked around helping the students begin. He didn't bother with the ones who clearly didn't want to be here.

As he helped a few of them begin their routines for this unit, Garth started to talk to them. Some of them seemed genuinely interested in wanting to be where Garth was, and they talked him up. For the first time, he compared arms with a few of them, showed them his thighs and forearms. He did not do any posing. These pups were so interested, and unlike some adults, they did not resent him for being where he was. They were full of drive to become something. They had no life experience that filled them with regret for wrong choices made or chances not taken. Garth was sure that was one of the dividing lines between puppyhood and adulthood.

Evan was still in good form today, performing flawless shrugs with weight he could handle. One of the other canines was watching Evan, a sandy-colored wolf. This caught Garth's eye, as the other canine was twice Evan's size. He seemed to be spotting for Evan. At one point, this wolf stood behind Evan and shadowed his movements. It looked like he was correcting pace, but at the same time they seemed close. A little too close. Evan's crotch looked nice and normal the whole time. Garth was relived, but at the same time he was also disappointed.

Finally it was time to send the students away to change. Garth followed them to the locker room and stepped into his miniscule office. Twenty extra workout papers lay on the desk. Garth filed them, then sat down in the chair and took a few deep breaths.

Locker room chatter rose, and then died off, and then the last bell rang. *Friday.*

Moments later, he heard the sound of running water around the corner. Garth sat up. Nobody used the showers after gym class. He stood up, pushing the chair against the wall and walked through the locker room to the shower area off to the far wall.

"Who's still here?"

No answer, but the water was running. Figuring some pup had turned on the water and run away, Garth walked down the stalls towards the sound. The showers were non-communal. Each head

49

had a stall separated by walls covered with the same tiles as the floor. He stopped at the second to last stall. Evan stood under the shower head, wearing only his gym shorts, fur soaked and matted down.

"Evan? What are you still doing here?"

Evan turned halfway around, leering at Garth. His bulge was beyond obscene in his wet gym shorts, and his cock was so blatantly outlined Garth could see the flare of the head. Garth felt his own crotch tighten in his shorts. As soon as he felt it, he turned around.

"Hurry up, Evan. School is out. You'll miss the bus."

"I don't live far away," the Doberman said. "I can walk."

"Why are you in there anyway?"

Evan giggled.

Garth was going to walk away, but he didn't move. He wanted to turn back around.

"Bet you look amazing after you shower," Evan said. "You know what the pups are saying about you?"

Garth had, but he wanted to hear what Evan had heard. "No, Evan. I don't."

"They're amazed you're here and not on stage at some competition. You should hear them. Coach Bob and Coach Bergeaud tried to get them on weights. Nobody did it. Then you give them the same weight routines the other two tried to give, and suddenly everyone wants to be in the gym. You're an inspiration to all the football and wrestling teams."

"That's why I'm here. Remember next week the workouts actually start. I'll be in the room most of the time."

The shower ran. Evan did not speak, and Garth couldn't tell what Evan was doing.

"Evan," Garth continued. "That's long enough. Get in the dryer so you don't miss the bus."

The water kept running. Garth wondered if Evan was just standing there, or if he was still there at all.

"Evan."

Garth turned his head. Evan was facing him directly, fur soaking wet, shorts clinging to him so tight he could see the pup's balls outlined. His cock hung halfway down to his knees. Garth did not turn away this time. Evan's smile crept up his muzzle.

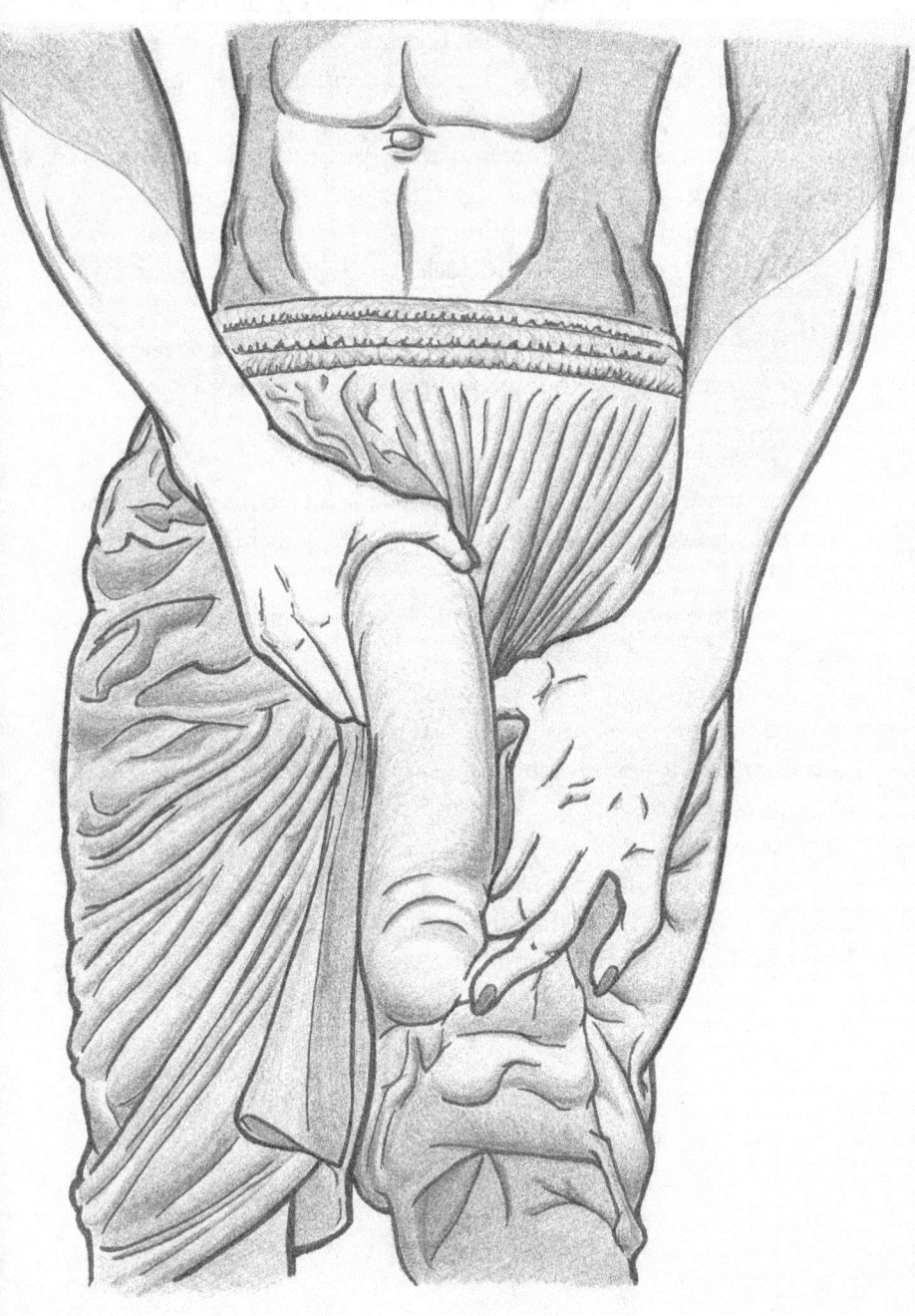

Evan shifted from paw to paw. His junk wiggled under the shorts. Garth was completely hard now. Evan's gaze zoomed in on it, and his smile grew. He stepped forward, out of the shower spray and walked up to Garth. Garth turned around to meet him as he approached.

The pup was about a foot shorter than Garth was, so when he entered Garth's personal space, his muzzle was lost in his chest. He was looking up at him, still smiling.

Garth felt a paw on his hard cock.

"Uh... Evan."

The paw rubbed up and down his dick and gave it a squeeze.

The next thing Garth knew his paw was squeezing Evan's limp cock.

Garth pulled away. "Shit, pup! Get out. Go home."

Evan never lost that predatory smile. He folded his paws behind his head, shook his hips, wagging his junk at Garth. Garth turned around.

"See you Monday, Mister Hood." Wet paws clicked away on the tile.

Garth waited until he was sure Evan was gone, and then he reached into the spray to shut the water off, only to realize this was an automatic shower. He stood there for a minute, letting the sound of running water hypnotize him, and sure enough the spray cut off on its own.

There was no sound of a dryer. Evan had left without drying his fur. Garth dreaded thinking about that poor pup walking around like that. That lucky, lucky pup.

Chapter 6

Garth was bare-chested at his computer desk, completely self-conscious of what he would look like to an outside observer, and wishing there were one. He was typing out a book report assignment. The students were to select a nonfiction book related to government, either buying it or borrowing it from the library. The topic could be anything from foreign policy to finance to internal issues to war. Garth wanted a full synopsis, summary of the issues presented, critical thinking of the topic presented. Choose an argument presented in the book and come up with a counterargument.

This would not be graded on a multiple guess sheet. This would require work that did not fit in the little boxes the computer required. This would require critical thinking, reading and a whole list of other skills. As long as Garth was in Government Studies, he should teach the pups something useful, and teach himself, too. These were seniors. They could handle it.

Garth paused, scratching his shoulder, biceps puckering his pecs. He smiled to himself, looking around his empty studio apartment. All of a sudden he missed having somebody to notice. He couldn't believe it had been two years. It was as if time had finally caught up to him.

He switched windows to the other thing he was doing when he had to break from the assignment: a job application.

When he graduated two years ago, Garth assumed people would come to him for his expertise. That's what the college recruiter told him in his freshman year of high school. *Get the right skills, they'll come to you.* In the last two years, he was lucky to get a rejection.

He had applied to multiple universities all over the country. Most never returned his application, but a few actually did send him a response which was always along the lines of: "thank you for your interest, but our physics department is full. We would normally be happy to take you on as an assistant, but you lack experience, so leave us alone." This had been going on for two solid years, from universities and the military to manufacturing and corporate labs.

Garth balked at the people on the news dismissing him as entitled and arrogant for not wanting to take a job in fast food or retail. Garth went to school to avoid such jobs because he was told he had to, and now people complained that he didn't want to do those jobs. Garth knew he was better than Golden Halo.

Now he was staring at the possibility of trying for retail. He knew damn well sure he was better than retail, and he didn't attend ten years of university to be manager at a Red Star department store, or employee of the month at a Music For You in a mall.

Garth leaned back in his computer chair, reassuring himself he did the right thing by moving. He had moved three times in two years, trying to follow the jobs. He moved close to a military base, close to labs, close to universities. If he hadn't done that, his leftover student loan money would have lasted another year, but he did what he knew was the right thing: follow the jobs, follow the jobs. This city was his last stop.

He wasn't useless, Garth kept telling himself. He wasn't whining. He had done everything he was supposed to. Employers were supposed to line up around the block to hire him. The college recruiter made it sound like that's exactly what would happen when he got a skill.

Instead, he lost a partner.

In the lonely hours of this afternoon with no place to go and nothing much to do, his thoughts often drifted back. It had only been two years, and he thought he would be broken up about it. Mostly, he felt guilt that he never had felt broken up by it.

He thought back on Clark. A fox, and also a weightlifter, but not nearly as into it as Garth had been, they could at least share the time in the gym together and they shared the same diet as well. The fox graduated first with a bachelor's degree. Garth remained in school for another six years, and Clark hung onto him.

What did Clark do with his degree his business? He had to take a job in a factory outside of town. No one was hiring, not even the retail places, and the fox refused to apply anywhere else because he didn't want to move and leave Garth. Then came Garth's turn to graduate the mastiff didn't want to end up like Clark, so Garth moved. The fox did not follow.

Garth did not miss Clark at all.

It had taken him the better part of a year to understand why he felt no sadness from the breakup. He never had felt much sadness leaving any of his previous mates. It was always Garth who broke up with them, and now that he took a step back from those situations, he understood why.

They were attracted to him, and he thought he was attracted to them, but it turned out that was the one thing that had been missing this whole time. The relationship was one-sided. They thought he was hot, and Garth mistook that for affection. Even after he got to know them, he still didn't feel very much for them, either physically or emotionally.

Two years by himself was what it took to help him realize that. They were attracted to him, but they had nothing that even remotely interested him. The relationships had their good times, and he did not dislike any of those guys, but he never truly felt anything for them.

All day while scoping out possibilities for jobs, Garth couldn't stop thinking about Evan. He questioned his memory, and more often than not his thoughts drifted to how he could see it again without getting into trouble.

The only time he saw something that perked his interest—the first time in his life he saw something *he* liked— and it was on a pup.

He raised his paw to his muzzle and closed his eyes.

"This is wrong."

He put it out of his mind and finished the application. He was sure he would come up empty, and he was shooting far beneath his college goal of *carpe lunam*. Then he switched back to the book report assignment and kept working on it. He added the following line to the requirements: *summarize the book so someone who has not read it can understand it.*

He went to bed, resolving to sit the pup down and tell him to back off.

Chapter 7

Garth caught up to Coach Campbell in the hall just outside the gymnasium, and walked beside the fox.

"Hey, Bob."

"Morning, Garth. How was your first week?"

"I feel so out of place. I dunno what I'm going to do when the gym unit ends."

Bob's ears twitched. "Follow the outline. It's all you gotta do."

"Do you have a minute? Can you tell me anything about one of your wrestling pups?"

"Maybe. Which one?"

"Evan Silvers."

The fox stopped walking and laughed, belly fat jiggling. Garth tried not to look.

"Evan, Evan, Evan. That pup. He's been on the team every year since he was a freshman."

"He seems a little uh... Forward."

"Been like that since middle school." He leaned close to Garth. "You see what he's packing?"

"No. Have you?"

"Only glimpses in the locker room. He is a freakin' showoff. Every chance he gets, he's waving it around. I tried to get him to stop, but you know what, ain't nobody ever bullied that pup. Everyone who tries, they never try it again. Can you guess why?"

"Why?"

Bob grinned, reached over, lifted Garth's ear up and whispered even quieter into it. "They give him trouble, he finds their girlfriends, shows them his dick, and suddenly their girl is all over him."

He let go of Garth's ear and moved back to normal conversation distance. "That's what I hear anyway. Never saw it go that far, but I do know all the assholes in the school leave him alone, and that's about the only reason I know."

"Wow," Garth said. "So how is he on the wrestling team?"

"He does all right. We made it to state level a couple years ago. Didn't win, but Evan was on the team and he did good."

"So how do you deal with him?"

"What do you mean?"

"I mean when he starts... *asserting* himself like that."

"What, on the other boys? You don't have to deal with anything, Garth. Pup has it under control. Everyone's afraid he'll take their girls away. Or beat them to death with his dick."

"He just seems a bit too confident to me. I worry someday it'll get him in trouble."

"He is too confident. Someday he'll learn, but if it keeps the bullies away I say it's a good thing. Half the time the bullies become his friends."

Coach Bob started walking down the hall again. Garth kept up.

"Shouldn't someone tell him? You can't just go waving your dick around to everybody?"

"Garth, if I had what that pup has, I'd be waving it around, too. I'd rub it in everyone's face."

"Hasn't anyone complained about Evan?"

Bob laughed again. "I've heard stories. Someone did complain, back when he was in eighth grade, maybe seventh. Not sure. Principal told me about it, 'cause I asked him about Evan, too. Pup was suspended out of school for two weeks, but you know what happened when he came back? That's when everyone left him alone. It got him respect, of all damned things, and they let him wave it around. Personally I think the boys get perverse pleasure from seeing it, and the girls get a kick out of watching their boys get all nervous. It never went that far again, but everyone knows about that pup. He doesn't even try to hide it." The fox smiled at Garth. "You see it?"

"No. He just seemed way too confident for his age. Also saw a couple bigger dogs hanging around him, looked so out of place."

"Count yourself lucky. It's ridiculous."

They had reached the gymnasium and walked in together. A few of the other coaches were here, standing against the bleachers, notepads and pencils in paw, whistles hanging around their necks.

Coach Jeremy yawned.

Coach Paul yawned right after the cat.

Then Coach Gary's mouth fell open.

The yawn spread among the entire group of coaches. Even Coach Bob caught it. Garth seemed to be immune. He looked up at the clock on the wall. Ten minutes to eight. Homeroom would let out any second, and first period would arrive five minutes later.

The yawn spread through the group of coaches again and again. Garth kept his distance so it wouldn't jump on him. He wished Sasha were here and not in the pool area. He couldn't believe he just came out to her like that last Friday. Campus was pretty open about it, but he'd been told it was a good idea to keep it to himself once he was out of school. So much for that plan, but he had the feeling she would be the best person to tell.

The bell rang. The hall filled with students. Very slowly, while the coaches made small talk, the students came in, wearing shorts and ready to be physical, even this early in the morning.

The yawn passed from coach to coach.

Finally the second bell rang, all the students were in shorts and loose shirts and milling around, waiting for attendance check. Garth did his students, and the other coaches did theirs.

Then Coach Paul blew his whistle, held his paws up. The students listened. "'K, listen everybody. First week of school is over. Today's a free day—" the students roared and cheered— "and, and I don't wanna see anybody standing around. Grab a basketball, grab a football, there's hockey equipment—" the students had already dispersed. Almost all of them went for the basketballs.

The coaches continued to yawn one after the other. Now free of the responsibility, they retreated to the locker rooms.

A student ran up to the mastiff, and Garth nodded to him. He was on the football team. "Mister Hood. We doin' weights today?"

Garth wanted to say yes, but instead he said, "Save your muscles for after school. Workouts begin this week, at least two per week. Don't forget to report to the nurse so she can weigh you. Fill out the paper, track your progress. Make sure the numbers are right. I will know if you're fudging them."

The pup smiled and nodded. "Right, Mister Hood."

"Have fun this period."

The dog ran off. Garth walked away, retreated to the locker rooms and confirmed what he already knew. The other coaches were playing games on their phones, or drinking coffee and munching on chips. Garth walked to his own office, sat down and thought about what a boring day this was going to be.

The next gym periods were just as boring. Garth wanted to pick up a basketball and join the pups, even though he wasn't much of a player himself, but it wouldn't be appropriate for a gym coach to actually play among the students. He always liked hockey and wondered if he would be any good at it. He smiled, thinking he would be the perfect goalie.

A number of his football and wrestling pups wanted Garth to check their forms right now, and he took them to the weight room and corrected them. While doing so, it occurred to Garth that if any of these players hurt themselves in the gym, it would come back on him, and with no actual qualifications, a single incident would mean the end of his job. He had to make this official, so he retreated to his office again and drew up some papers about proper form and preventing injury. He then took them to the copy room and ordered three hundred. He would make every pup in his class sign off on them, so if there were any injuries, he could at least prove that he did provide proper instruction.

They could still fire him anyway for the lack of qualifications thing, but he might avoid a civil suit. Garth thought he was being paranoid, but perhaps it was wise to cover his ass around here.

When Government Studies came around, Garth changed into his teacher clothes and fought the urge to declare it a free day. He did not do a class lecture today. Instead, he handed out the book report assignment.

"Pick a nonfiction book from the library or buy one. Either way, there are a ton of books about government and the topics are endless. Pick a topic that interests you. Like... Shelly. What topic interests you?"

Shelly was a yellow lab in the second row. Garth picked her because she looked the most like she wanted to be on her phone texting. She shrugged.

"Nothing yet," Garth said. "That's fine. Pick a topic. Pick many topics. You may find something that interests you. That's what school is for."

Garth went over his list of suggested authors to investigate. He encouraged the students to probe the topics they wrote about, read excerpts from the book, find something that seemed interesting.

"This assignment will be much more pleasant if you choose a book you're interested in."

He'd spent the first half hour of class discussing the book report, giving the students ideas for how to search for something, how to choose a book. He wanted them to have a book by the end of the week, and he wanted them to finish the report by the end of the month. It was plenty of time for an assignment like this, but of course the high-schoolers whined that it couldn't possibly be enough time to do a project this big. Garth smiled and laughed.

He assigned them today's chapter in the textbook as homework, and gave them the rest of the period. Garth felt good about himself. He had broken up the routine he was falling into, broken out of the class outline and mere teaching the textbook and given the students something that required effort.

His second period of government began, and Evan was very quiet. He didn't look at Garth once, and he appeared to take on the same wish-I-were-texting attitude as the rest of the students. Garth made it through his entire discussion on the book report without once thinking about the puppy.

Finally, last period. He changed back into a gym coach, the other coaches declared another free day and disappeared, and Garth found himself in the gymnasium, alone. As the last coach to leave, he was stuck as chaperone.

Evan walked up to him, holding a soccer ball. Once again, his crotch was obscene, and Garth couldn't help but stare.

"Mister Hood. No weights today?"

Garth wasn't going to play this game. "Come with me, Evan."

He held the soccer ball and followed the mastiff to the locker rooms, and into his office. Garth sat at the desk, and Evan stood in the corner, as there was no room to be behind the desk. Evan pulled the door closed behind him.

"Evan, don't do that again."

The dobie smiled.

"I mean it, Evan. You could get in serious trouble. I could get in serious trouble. Coach Bob told me all about you. Now nobody else seems to have the guts to say it but I will, and I don't mean this as a teacher. I mean this as someone who's been out in the world. You keep doing stuff like this, and you will get in big trouble."

Evan's smile never faded. It was annoying.

"Listen to me, Evan. From now on, hands off, and keep your junk as visible as possible—*invisible* as possible!"

Evan laughed, dropped the soccer ball and held his shorts at the waist.

"You wanna see it again?"

"Evan, no."

"Then why didn't you invite another coach in the room with us?"

"I don't want to embarrass either of us," Garth said, but as he said it he realized he had messed up. The professional thing to do was partner up with somebody so there would be a witness.

"I can smell it. Oh, I hoped you'd want to see it. Everyone does once."

He pulled his shorts down. His cock dangled halfway to his knees, swinging freely. Evan held his arms up, funneling Garth's vision to it. Garth opened his mouth and tried to speak, but nothing came out. Evan swung his hips back and forth, smacking each thigh with his cock. Evan picked it up and waved it around clockwise, still smiling.

"Damn, pup. That's... That's..."

Evan stepped the two paces over to Garth. His hips were close to Garth's eye level, and Evan held the tip up to Garth's nose. Impulsively, he sniffed it, and then turned away.

"It's okay," Evan said. "I don't mind."

"Evan, this is bad."

"Well I have good news for you," Evan said. "I just turned eighteen."

All of a sudden Garth didn't feel the student/teacher barrier between him and Evan. It was staring Garth in the face. It was the first time Garth looked at someone and felt any kind of excitement. With Clark and all his previous relationships, arousal had come from seeing them satisfied. Evan was someone he wanted for himself.

Garth reached up, wrapped his fingers around Evan's shaft and suckled on the head. The mastiff felt it quickly expanded in his paw, the girth spreading his fingers out. Evan rubbed his forearm, feeling the separation between the muscles. The dobie's paw slid up the arm and upon feeling the bicep Evan's cock ballooned instantly. Garth held onto it as it filled his muzzle. It tasted so good, and Garth had never enjoyed giving head before. He had been strictly a fuck or get fucked kind of dog, and that he was enjoying this, eyes closed and everything, was entirely new. Evan kept his voice down, but he couldn't stop his erratic breathing.

Finally the Doberman's cock was all the way up and Garth released it, held it at a distance and took a moment to admire why everybody left him alone. He was no shop teacher, so he couldn't measure with his eyes, but Evan's dick was too big to be real. It should not exist, especially not on this pup. Garth had large paws, and it would take four to cover Evan.

He simply held it with both paws. Garth's shorts were soaked with pre already, and he had not even touched himself. Evan leaned over to be at Garth's eye level while he reached up and felt both of Garth's arms. Garth leaned back and let the pup feel the rest of him. He was used to this. It was all Clark and his previous relationships had done. Their pleasure had given him pleasure, or so he'd thought.

And the dobie was smiling like a predator that had just caught his prey. Garth felt a hand on his crotch. The pup was squeezing it, and confirming Garth was hard made the smile somehow even more conquering. He was undoing Garth's pants. Garth turned to the door, trying to see through it and figure out if anyone knew they were in here, but before he could figure it out, Evan had Garth's pants undone and was already on his knees.

Evan sucked dick like he was born to. The whole time he was feeling up Garth's arms, and Garth flexed for him, giving him more territory to explore. Evan's paws wandered down and felt Garth's thighs, gripping them, testing them, admiring how solid and thick they were. He tried to wrap his hands around Garth's thigh, and two of Evan's hands would not even grip halfway around it. As Evan felt this, his muzzle worked more magic on Garth.

The mastiff strained to stay silent. He looked down, admiring how a dobie this young could be so good at this. He caught glimpses of Evan's dick from here, and just the sight of it made Garth want to cum. Imagining this little dobie with a rod that size blew Garth's mind. Thinking about it made his hips buck and magnified the motions of Evan's tongue.

Evan shifted position, knelt with Garth's cock all the way down his muzzle, paws wandering from his thick thighs up to his abs. His eyes were open, and he was looking up at Garth. Garth leaned back in the chair, letting his chest hide his face from view. Even with a shirt on, his pecs were still a sight. It must have worked on Evan, as now his tongue and muzzle made him feel better than ever. Garth leaned even further back, panting and squeezing the armrests. Evan's paw wandered to his forearms to catch the action.

Evan moved his muzzle back and forth, working the entire shaft with his tongue, teasing the head at random moments. Garth never knew when it was coming, so when it did, it caught him off guard every time, and he strained to hold it in. He felt two paws on his abs, which wandered around and tried to feel Garth's rear. He would have been happy to let Evan go that far, but Evan's muzzle kept him pinned to the chair.

Garth screamed in strained silence. He couldn't hold it anymore. As he held his muzzle shut, his cock pulsed as hot cum rushed up it. Evan lapped it up, paw feeling Garth's flexed arms all the way around. Garth had never finished that fast before. Garth leaned forward and looked down at Evan as the pup milked the last drops out of it. He almost felt bad for not warning Evan, but the dobie did not look offended.

As soon as he was dry, Evan released Garth and rose to full height. Garth felt a little lightheaded and simply stared at Evan's dick. Evan gripped it once, squeezed it and milked the biggest wad of pre Garth had ever seen. Garth reached up, grabbed it and lapped it up. Evan shoved it back into Garth's muzzle.

Now Garth suckled it as best as he could. It was too large to take all the way, but Garth tried. Something about it... he wanted to take it all, but he could only do about half of it before the girth spread his muzzle too far. Evan's quick breathing reassured him that halfway was more than enough.

Evan's paws explored Garth's upper body, feeling every crevice he had only been able to imagine from a distance. Garth now wished he had removed his shirt for the pup, as he clearly wanted to know what was under it. He was feeling it hard enough, hands on his pecs, admiring they were each larger than his entire hand could span.

Garth had only been suckling it for a minute when Evan started thrusting and moaning. He tapped Garth's pec a few times, and Garth held on. Evan pulsed and warm liquid gushed down his muzzle.

Evan finished much too fast, and Garth wondered if his muzzle had anything to do with it, or if being able to touch what he had admired for so long was enough. Garth sucked it all down as the pup felt him up. When he began to go soft, Evan pulled out and sat on Garth's lap, grinding the mastiff's limp cock between his cheeks. He sat muzzle to muzzle with Garth, wrapped his arms around him, pushed an ear up with his nose and whispered.

"I've had dreams about you."

Garth didn't know what to say, but his paw reached around and held the pup's rear, giving it a payback squeeze. Evan giggled.

"Oh my God, this is wrong," Garth whispered back.

"I really am eighteen, had my birthday two months ago."

"Someone must have seen us. They'll know. They'll find out. Oh, shit, Evan, we're both gonna get it."

Evan lowered his muzzle down to Garth's and licked it. Garth kissed back. It was the most passionate kiss Garth ever shared.

Moments later, the bell rang.

"Shit," Garth said. "You're due for wrestling practice and a workout. I'm working with Bob."

"Good," Evan said. "Spot me. I'll be doing upper body."

He patted Garth's pec, squeezed it, growled, leaned close and kissed Garth again. It lasted for another minute. Then he got up, and pulled his shorts back on. Garth re-buttoned his pants. They were both still panting.

"See you soon, Garth," Evan said.

"Yeah. You, too Evan."

The dobie opened the door and walked out. Garth sat in the chair and slouched. He still wasn't sure if it had happened, but the cum sizzled in his stomach, so it must have.

He snuck to the restroom and straightened his clothes and fur as best as he could. Then he took a few deep breaths, left the lockers and headed straight for the weight room. Then he remembered the paper he had dropped off earlier and wondered if it would be ready now, so he walked to the offices where the copy machine was and found his stack. Now it was time to make it official.

He took the ream of forms and carried them to his office, where he grabbed a box of pens and carried all of it to the gymnasium. Coach Bob and Coach Joey were waiting for him. They had extended one bleacher out to form a table, and several stacks of papers were there. Paul was on the other side of the gym, talking to a few of his students.

The fox yawned again. The husky yawned, too. Garth rolled his eyes, turned his head to the side and set his ream next to others and joined the coaches as they waited for everyone to arrive.

Students were arriving and they formed a little cluster around the coaches, waiting for instructions. Evan came from the hallway, now dressed in more modest clothes, and stood amongst the crowd. Garth tried not to look at him.

Once the traffic in the hall died down, Garth was sure they had their group. Garth and the other coaches had already worked out a schedule, balancing weight room with practice, and now it was time to get everyone started.

Joey blew his whistle and instructed everyone to take a workout/practice schedule. Then Garth spoke up and told everyone the other form was an explanation of injury prevention and workout safety. Everyone was to take one, read it, sign it, date it, and give it to him. If there were any questions, ask him. He wanted everyone to be safe doing these workouts.

The students took their papers. Some read the form, others did not, but they signed it and that was all that mattered to Garth. Now there was documentation that he was doing his job.

With the schedule set, Joey and Bob took their students for practice, and Garth took his batch to the weight room. Now Garth was glad he had assigned some students upper body and others lower body, because the school's gym was full. Garth wasn't sure what his role would be, but as he walked around the room, he found himself playing personal trainer to everyone. Most of them were just starting, Garth kept an eye out for rookie mistakes.

He saw a feline on the football team perform military presses, arching his back way too far.

"John!" Garth shouted.

The feline faced him and paused before he did another rep.

"You're using too much weight. You're going to hurt yourself if you do that."

The feline nodded. Garth breathed a little easier, but wondered how it was possible for anyone to mess up like that. Too much weight should be obvious.

Ten minutes later Garth caught two wrestlers trying to compete in one-legged squats. Garth blew his whistle for the first time and broke it up right away.

"This is not playtime!" Garth growled at both of them. Then he turned to the whole gym. "Everyone, stick to the moves I showed you. Keep your form right, and do not try to get clever. You could hurt yourself."

Nobody spoke. The pups resumed their workouts, and Garth scanned the room, watching them. Garth wasn't too much older than these students, but even when he first started with weights he knew he could hurt himself if he did anything wrong, so he never played around.

Then again, he was alone. These pups were on teams, they knew each other, and they were watching each other. Garth had explained over and over to lift at their own level, don't try to compete with anyone, but the urge to compete made them do dumb things.

Garth had been the one to suggest keeping people from the same team out of the weight room, so the students could focus on the weights and not talking about the game, or practice, or about the coaches. He wondered how much worse things would be if he hadn't suggested that.

Evan was in good form. His curls were textbook and even his tricep extensions were superb. He wanted to compliment Evan and use him as the example of proper form to the rest of the group, but now did not seem like the best time to draw attention to him. When Evan moved to bench, one of the larger canines from the football team spotted for him. Garth wondered why this dog would spot for Evan.

Garth looked at the clock. Twenty minutes had gone by.

"All right, everybody, pace yourselves. A workout only needs to last half an hour to forty-five minutes. If you're not halfway done by now, pick up the pace. Don't worry if you run short on time. You'll learn to pace yourself as you practice."

The students dutifully wrote down their moves, weights, sets and reps information on the forms he had handed out during regular gym class. It was good to be among a group of people who wanted to be here, who wanted to work their bodies.

Garth checked forms, gave advice, suggested more weight or less weight for the next half hour. By the end, it was time to hand them back to the coaches and take the next batch.

Garth did not want to make the pups do a workout after football or wrestling practice, but the coaches insisted they had to make the most of their time. Garth had to relent, but he made the coaches promise not to wear the pups out on their B-shift workout days.

To Garth's relief, Evan ran off with the others and met up with Coach Bob on the mats for wrestling practice. Garth hoped Bob wouldn't overwork the pups who just finished a workout.

The whole schedule was not to Garth's liking. Ideally, there should be a workout, or a practice session, and that would be it, but they had to do something to fill the time between now and when the late busses arrived, so the best plan was to have two shifts of students per day, one doing a workout for an hour, the other doing practice for an hour. Garth feared the extra effort would cancel out any gains they were supposed to make.

He supervised the next batch of students, wearing himself out correcting their rookie mistakes in posture. Five minutes into class Garth caught one student loading a barbell up with too much weight. Garth walked over to him. A student was set to spot for him, but Garth stepped over the bench and did it for him.

The canine picked up the weight, Garth held it. Sure enough, it was too much, and the canine struggled to hold it up. Garth held it for him, getting an unintended lat workout.

"Feel that?" Garth said, loud enough for everybody to hear.

The canine under the barbell nodded.

"That's what too much weight feels like. You're just starting out. You can't bench one-fifty yet. Start with sixty, see how that works. Don't try to compete with anyone, especially me. Don't try to be a big dog by lifting more than you can. You'll just end up at the hospital."

Garth lifted the barbell out of the canine's paws and set it on the rack. The student sat up, swiveled halfway around and faced Garth.

"Understand?" said the mastiff.

"Right, Mister Hood."

"Good. Now load up the barbell with the right amount of weight and try again."

Garth walked away, scanned the rest of the room for more pups trying to be bigger than they were. The canine at the bench loaded the barbell with two ten pound weights on either side and tried again. It was too little, and he loaded it with seventy. That seemed right. When he finished a set, Garth nodded to him and gave him a thumbs up. The dog didn't seem embarrassed by how little he could bench now.

The others in the room had taken that lesson as if they had been the ones lying on that bench, and most everyone was in good form now. Some asked him questions. Garth helped others find a good weight for them.

Some of the students took his advice and brought protein powder as a post-workout drink. Others just took water, and Garth hoped they had good dinners waiting for them at home.

At four-thirty, the late busses arrived, and after a quick attendance check, the students were dismissed. Garth caught Evan's eye. The dobie was still smiling at him. Garth's crotch tightened and he averted his gaze. He wanted to pull the pup aside and talk to him, but he thought he had taken enough risks today. The dobie winked at him, and then merged with the crowd of students going home.

Someone smacked Garth on the shoulder and held him.

"See?" Bob said, pulling up to Garth shoulder to shoulder. "Told ya it would work just fine. The pups can handle a workout and practice a couple times a week. And you should hear what they say about you behind your back."

Garth smiled. "Do tell."

"I think you could tell them to wash toilets all period and they'd do it if they thought it would help them end up like you someday."

"Don't give the bosses any ideas," Garth said.

"Hell, no. Ready for another group?"

"Yup, I think it'll get easier once they have a routine. I won't have to watch them every second."

"Don't admit that too loud," Bob said, ears back, tail waving. "Lilith will find something else for you to do."

He let go of Garth's shoulder and walked away from him. Garth sighed, picked up his stack of papers and retreated to his office. Inside, he paused. He looked behind the door. Nobody was there. He expected Evan to be waiting for him. He breathed easier knowing he was alone.

"Shit," he said. "That was wrong, but fucking hot."

Chapter 8

Tuesday was a repeat of Monday, but without the blowjob, and with surprisingly little leering from the dobie. Garth was glad the pup didn't have a workout day today. He and the other coaches had worked it out so each student would have at least a day between workouts.

Garth watched the Tuesday groups even more closely. He was sure they had been talking to each other, and yet he still caught some of the jocks trying to lift more than they could, or trying to invent a game at the squat rack.

One canine on the leg press machine was trying to do shoulders on it, and two other jocks were laughing, egging him on. Garth rushed in, held the rack up and told the student to get out.

Garth announced if he caught anyone fooling around on the equipment again, he would kick them out of the weight room, and it would be up to their coach whether they would stay on the team. Garth didn't think he had it in him to be this harsh and authoritative, but he was scared at just how stupid these pups were. As often as he explained this was not playground equipment, they did not seem to get it. He was afraid to turn his back on them. He was sure if he could get everyone in the gym, alone, without their friends looking at them while they worked out, they would be models of safety and their apparent maturity would be through the roof.

As Garth observed them for the last half hour, he thought about Evan. The dobie hadn't spoken to him all day, and that's what surprised Garth most. Evan seemed to be keeping it together very well, but every time Garth saw the pup, his crotch tightened and he had to adjust himself. Every time Evan looked at him, Garth had to think about Lilith Dover to keep it down.

He wanted to ask other teachers about Evan, but he had not had much time during the day to wander around and talk to other teachers. Plus, he figured asking around about a particular student would look suspicious, and the best thing to do was not draw attention to himself.

There had been no time to read the next chapter in his government textbook and prepare a lecture, so once again Garth had to read from the book. The students were uninterested, and Garth assigned the quiz at the end of the book for the remainder of class and it kept everyone occupied.

Wednesday was the same as Tuesday, except this time he couldn't be in the weight room. As the last bell rang and Garth changed out of his teacher clothes, his heart raced. The last two days he had to watch those pups like a security camera or they would do something stupid. Now he couldn't be there because he had Student Council. He stopped in the gym one last time and found Joey, the Husky wrestling coach, standing in the middle of the weight room.

"Joey," Garth said. "Remember what I told you. Watch them. Make sure they don't play around or try to lift more than they can handle."

Joey nodded, but his face seemed distant. "I'll make sure."

"Please do. I'll see you tomorrow. Tell me everything."

Garth speed walked to his Government Studies classroom, sat behind the desk and waited for everyone to arrive. He leaned back in his chair and read the list of issues he was supposed to bring up to the group.

The *congress,* as it was titled at the top of the page. Garth rolled his eyes and read. On it were exceptionally important topics such as allocation of soda machine duty, whether the vending machines in the cafeteria should offer all-natural snacks and beverages, the issue of whether there should be an alternative lunch offered for the felines.

Garth lowered the paper, stared at the far wall and thought about that one. How many felines were in this school? They couldn't digest plants as well as canines could, and when he was in high school, felines had their own lunches. It was usually cheap, canned fish, but it wasn't blended with soy like most red meat was, so at least they could eat it. Was that no longer true? Garth was sure they were smart enough to bring their own food, but why wouldn't the school offer something they could eat?

Garth looked at the paper again and read the last item, whether the cafeteria should offer metal utensils instead of the disposable plastic ones.

Included on the list was his role in the discussion. He was supposed to "raise the issue, present the merits of each decision and the potential consequences thereof, as noted below."

Garth read it. Much like the educator's edition textbooks, there were suggested scripts for him to say.

On filling the soda machines: "Hard work may not be rewarded directly, but it can have various social consequences that benefit others."

On the vending machines and healthy alternatives: "Providing an informed public wise choices is an essential function of a governing body, however, one must also weigh the costs with expected returns."

On the alternative lunch for the felines point: "The purpose of a governing body is to weigh costs with benefits while encouraging people to take responsibility for themselves."

On the utensil point: "Remember to weigh the cost of labor against the cost of waste disposal."

After he was done, he wondered if he should have been required to sign a nondisclosure form for this class as well. Apparently, his job was to push someone's political agenda on the Student Council, not encourage them to make a decision. Then he realized it was in his best interest to push the Council into making the easiest choice for him to execute, as he had little time to do anything else.

One by one the students began arriving. Second to walk through the door was Evan Silvers. Garth's heart stopped and his crotch tightened. The dobie smiled.

"Evan, you're on Student Council, too?"

"I heard my weight room coach was in charge of it, so I volunteered to represent my class."

Garth smiled. "Coach Bob okay letting you go for a practice?"

"Student Council is only once a week. I don't have to be in wrestling practice every night."

"Well, get ready for a real lesson in how government works."

"Are we going to vote on stuff today?"

"Oh yeah. I've got a list of issues for the group right here."

Evan smiled. He adjusted himself under his desk and sat with his legs spread apart. Garth could see the outline of the monster resting beside his left leg. Garth tried not to look, and he wanted to stare at it all night long.

There were eight students on the Council altogether, two from each grade. According to the paper he found in his mailbox in the office, once everyone had a seat and introductions were out of the way, Garth's first duty was to introduce the Council and its purpose. Most of the students had been on it last year, so they knew how it worked.

Garth proposed the utensil point first, ignoring the script until he heard what the students thought of the matter.

One female boxer, Gina, had a lot to say on the topic. Garth didn't think it was possible to have a debate about the merits of plastic utensils over metal, but she had a very strong opinion on the subject, rooted in teenage overconfidence and untainted by the realities of logistics. She wanted to save the environment, plastic was evil, so the decision was obvious.

The students agreed, all around the room. It seemed to be the only conclusion possible. This was Garth's cue to inject a little reality into the debate.

"All of you have made good points," he said. "I'm curious do any of you have part-time jobs outside of school?"

Only one canine raised his hand.

"I thought so. None of you have any work experience so you wouldn't think of this. Let's say the school does get metal forks, spoons and knives. Who's going to wash them? The cafeteria staff already has enough to do without figuring out when they're going to wash several thousand pieces of silverware every day. This is why the school uses disposable utensils in the first place."

"Well, we can hire a dishwasher," said Gina, "or get a student to volunteer for the job."

"Will you volunteer for it?" Garth said. "I promise the school won't hire someone just to wash spoons all day."

"How 'bout a dishwasher?" one of the males in the back said.

"The cafeteria already has a couple, and they're at capacity. There is no room for another unit," Garth said. He didn't actually know this, but he was willing to place money on it.

"So there's no choice?" Evan said. Under his desk, he scratched his leg, which made his limp dick wiggle around under the fabric. He pulled his pants tighter, making it even more obvious.

Garth smiled, and kept his eyes on the dobie's. "Not this time. This point was to help you pups see there are more dimensions to an issue than it appears. Always try to see things from multiple points of view."

The other points were the same way. About the alternative lunch options, the students were adamant that everyone should be considered, and then Garth injected his script into the conversation and it effectively deflated the debate.

The same thing happened at the alternative snack option for the vending machines. Everyone wanted more choices, until Garth's script told them they did not sell as well, so it was in the school's best interest to stock what sold.

Finally came the soda machine duty. Someone had to volunteer to give up a study hall to stock the soda machines, and Garth couldn't believe the students were actually doing it. They saw it as helping their school, not the school being cheap and pushing a menial task on someone who would do it for free.

Garth was relieved they didn't make a decision that he had to execute. He watched the students leave. Just before the dobie was out the door, Garth spoke.

"Oh, Evan," he said.

The pup stopped at the door, holding both straps of his backpack.

"I need to talk to you real quick."

The pups filed out past him, and when he was the last student left in the room, Garth spoke again.

"Close the door, please."

Evan did, gently, then walked up to Garth's desk and sat down on it. Garth was now at eye level with Evan's waist. The pup had sat so his cock was resting down one thigh, puckering the fabric up. Garth kept his eyes on Evan's.

"We can't let that happen again," Garth said.

Evan said nothing, but continued smiling and sitting with his pants accentuating his penis outline.

"I'm serious, Evan. Yesterday was a mistake. It really was. We could both get in a lot of trouble."

Evan's smile spread into a grin.

"I don't think you realize just how serious this is. Eighteen or not, you're still a student, and I'm a teacher."

Evan leaned over, sprawling on Garth's desk sideways, grabbed his cock through his pants and shook it a bit. Garth couldn't help but stare at it, and then he looked up at Evan's grinning muzzle again.

"Stop that, Evan," Garth said, trying not to raise his voice. "I'm serious. I don't want you to get hurt by this, and I—"

As he spoke, Evan unbuttoned his pants and pushed them down just far enough for him to take it out and wave it in front of Garth. The physicist glanced at the door to confirm nobody could see the desk from here, and then he faced Evan, making sure to look only at his muzzle.

"This is beyond inappropriate. You shouldn't be doing this, especially to me, not to mention the other students."

Evan's cock was growing, and now Garth got a full view of it. The thing reached Evan's chest in this position, and the mastiff wondered how it could get all the way hard. Evan seemed to recognize Garth was trying to figure it out, adjusted himself and gripped it with both paws, just to show how much room there was. It was longer than Garth's forearm.

"Put that away before someone walks in on you!"

"No one would care," Evan said, rubbing himself up and down with both paws at once.

"You bet your ass they would. I could get in serious trouble. You flash that thing to the wrong person you'll end up in court."

"I've flashed it to every pup in school. No trouble yet."

"I'm not a puppy."

"You're also the hottest dog I've ever met," Evan said, licking his lips. His paws squeezed pre from his tip. He kept rubbing. "I cammed with a couple dogs almost as big as you, but I never thought I'd ever meet someone like you in real life."

Garth was following Evan's hands with his eyes. He had never seen anyone whack off with two paws before, and with so much room to spare. Evan continued.

"When I was a freshman, a new feline moved here. Big cat. Didn't even work out and he was huge. He thought it would be fun to start picking on me and a couple other dogs. Kept shoving us into lockers as he walked by, pretending it was an accident. Wasn't long before he had a girlfriend."

Evan shifted around, moved up to the edge of the desk, reached out with one paw and rested it on Garth's chest.

"Damn, you're huge," he said. "And solid!" He patted Garth's pec, squeezed it. His cock seemed to stiffen even more and he rubbed himself faster. "That cat could've been like you if he started lifting. So one day I found him walking with his girlfriend in the hallway. There was a crowd around us, 'cause it was between classes. I didn't say anything. Just stood there, waved to them, and whipped it out. The look on her face... the look on *his*!"

Evan rolled over, sat up in front of Garth, his legs dangling off the desk, his cock upright and poking Garth's chin. He leaned back, and kept rubbing himself while groping Garth's bicep and tricep, marveling that he couldn't wrap his hand around it. More pre oozed out of his tip and he used it as lube, rubbing himself faster and faster.

"He found me again after school. There was something different about him that time. I could tell. He really wanted to see it again. He practically begged me to show it to him, hard this time. So I did. And he starts blowing me. He looked out for me after that. Someone else gave me a hard time, he would set them straight. Never saw him with that female again, but he sure kept me safe until he moved. Wish he hadn't. I liked him. He gave good head, and he was a great fuck."

Evan's hands had been exploring Garth's chest and arms. Garth had been sitting still, mesmerized by the sight of this monster staring at him. More and more precum squeezed out and now the pup was so slick his paw glided over it with no effort at all.

"He wasn't the first person I did that to," Evan said. "It's made me a lot of friends over the years. Some who'd rather I stay away from them. Some who want me close, but can't."

His paw wandered up to Garth's muzzle. This startled Garth, who looked up from Evan's oozing tip and met the canine in the eye.

"But this is the first time I've met someone *I* wanted," Evan said. "I've only seen people like you in magazines. I didn't know you existed in real life, and that you'd come here! Soon as I figured you'd... be interested... I knew I had to..."

His breath was short, and Garth smelled climax. Evan gestured for him to come closer. Garth instinctually leaned over, gripped Evan's cock and suckled the tip. Evan rubbed himself with both paws, eyes on Garth's bent arm as the mastiff's forearm muscle pushed his bicep up. Evan held both his paws together at the base of his dick, which pulsed in Garth's paw as hot jizz spilled into his muzzle. Garth lapped it up and swallowed. His other paw came up and felt Evan's meat. It was still slick, and his paws traveled up and down it with no resistance. The pup seemed to cum endlessly, and Garth lapped it up.

Finally Evan sat up, leaned closer and licked the side of Garth's muzzle. Garth released Evan's cock and looked him in the eye. Evan's smile was gentle all of a sudden. He licked Garth's muzzle a few more times. Garth licked him back once.

"Uh..." Garth trailed off, unsure how to continue.

"I'll bring lube next time. I want you to fuck my brains out."

Evan wasn't even close to soft yet and he slid off the desk and stood up.

"Evan, we can't do this."

Evan stood there, cock slowly going limp and dripping leftover cum on the floor. He laughed. "You don't seem to mind."

"I could be fired. You could be kicked out of school. You don't want to mess up your life like that. I don't."

"It's all gym coaches, Mister Hood. You think they care about what I do? They've had since middle school to kick me out."

"That doesn't mean you're safe."

Evan smiled, eyes darting to both of Garth's arms. Garth realized the way he was sitting in the chair made his arms and chest pucker out. Evan raised his arms and did a double bicep pose. His smile rose into a grin. "You are amazing! I can't wait for you to fuck me. Wish I brought the lube today, but I didn't want to be too pushy."

Garth laughed a little, gestured to Evan's crotch, which had finally shrunk down most of the way, but it was still twice as long as Garth's, even when all the way up. Evan stuffed it down his pants and walked to the door.

"See you tomorrow."

"Yeah... Bye, Evan."

With one last smile, Evan opened the door and left, shutting it behind him. Garth was glad for that; as soon as the pup was gone, Garth undid his pants, whipped his cock out, grabbed a few tissues and finished in ten seconds. He wadded it all up, wiped the jizz from the floor, walked to one of the bathrooms in the hall and dropped everything in the trash.

He stood looking in the mirror. He was hard again, and Garth grabbed himself and whacked off a second time.

Chapter 9

Terrance, the fat mastiff who coached basketball and economics, stood before all the students in first period. Garth hadn't seen him since school began and wondered where he had been all this time.

"Free day everyone."

The students did not seem excited by this, as if it were old news and someone had just told it to them for the third time.

Because they had. This was the third free day the coaches had declared this week, and it was only Thursday. Most of the students grabbed basketballs. Some just sat on the partially-extended bleachers and did homework.

The gym coaches meanwhile, sat around and talked amongst themselves. Garth hung his head and growled. Before the students got started, Garth blew his whistle and held up his arms.

"If anyone wants to get some weightlifting in, meet me in the gym."

He lowered his arms and walked through the middle of the gymnasium, around some of the students dribbling basketballs and trying to shoot hoops. Terrance was on the sideline, watching them.

Garth walked into the weight room, turned around and waited. To his surprise, five students followed him. Garth was relieved there were still people in this school who weren't lazy.

They had their papers with them, and some were moving to the lower body machines, others to the upper body. Garth watched them for a few minutes, walked around, and started speaking to them. There were fewer students now, and he had a chance to talk to them. Ask if they wanted to get serious about working out, if they knew what was involved in it.

Others heard them, and Garth had a conversation with everyone as they worked out. They asked him what was really involved in getting to the level he was. They asked him why he did it.

Garth didn't want to reveal his real major, but he did feel free to say one thing. "I enjoy it. I enjoy being physical. I kept it up all the years I was in college."

The students laughed.

Garth grinned at them. "You're laughing, but let me make sure you're not just hiding insecurity. Don't be ashamed of how much or how little you can bench or curl. That's your level. You can raise it any time. Don't compare yourself to me and think you can never be where I am. Anything is possible."

Garth always felt like he could never say it enough. Today he added something new.

"Evan, when you're in college studying to become a computer technician or something, you can keep up with this. It's an old cliché that you have to be a meathead to get like this. It's almost true, but you can be the exception."

Some students seemed to take everything he said as gospel. He enjoyed it with the abbreviated groups he had for the next four periods, until his lunch. He left the gymnasium, walked the hall to the teacher's lounge. He passed the cafeteria, and paused. The chatter was light, but growing.

Garth veered off course and walked into the cafeteria. First lunch period was just beginning, and the students were filing in, getting in line for food. Garth stepped in line without a tray and moved through it, just looking at what they had to offer.

To Garth's surprise, about the only thing they offered was red meat for canines covered in gravy. It may have been soup, or stew, or meatloaf. Further down the line were some empty serving trays. Behind the counter, the kitchen staff was working at ovens. Garth was right; there was no room in here whatsoever for an extra dishwasher, packed as it was with ovens and sinks, and even with only two canines working back there, it was cramped.

One of the canines with white fur was walking up to the line with a bowl. She poured it into one of the empty serving trays and was about to turn around.

"Excuse me," Garth said.

The canine reacted as if she hadn't been spoken to in centuries. She stopped, slowly turned her muzzle up, faced Garth and took a moment to remember how to speak. "Yes?"

"What was that?"

"Cream corn."

Garth looked down at it. He would have sworn it was cream of mushroom soup. He met the canine's eyes again.

"If I were a cat, what would I have to choose from?"

She laughed, shook her head. "Not much anymore. The meat's blended with so much soy I don't know how any of the cats handle it. Most don't even try. Even when it wasn't blended they wouldn't touch the stuff."

"When I was in school, cats had their own selection. What happened to that?"

"Same reason we only have three people on staff back here. We used to have six."

"Gotya. Are there a lot of felines in this school?"

"Eh, not that many, but enough. One in ten I'd say."

"Doesn't the school offer anything for them? Fish? Something not blended with soy and covered in mushroom soup or gravy?"

The canine shook her head. "Too expensive, even the blended meat is expensive. We're lucky to have this. Things keep going this way the students will be down to bread and water, and they'll have to buy their water from the vending machines."

"Wow. Thanks."

She smiled at him, nodded good-day, and returned to the kitchen. Garth stepped out of line and walked back through the cafeteria. If he were a feline, he'd feel left out. Even as a canine, he wouldn't touch any of the stuff in those trays.

He walked by the vending machines and paused to look inside. They were packed with candy bars, bags of chips and little else. No gum, of course. A glance at the soda machines made him do a double take. It was stocked entirely with sports water. It may have had electrolytes, but it was still mostly sugar. Garth shook his head and was about to walk out when he caught a scent and turned around.

Evan was in the lunch line, standing hip to hip with a large canine one whole head taller than he was. Evan was looking at Garth. Even from here, Garth could make out his smile. Garth turned around and slipped out of the cafeteria and walked to the lounge. He fetched his lunch from one of the refrigerators and walked back to the gymnasium to eat lunch in his locker room office. Suddenly he didn't want to be alone. On a whim, Garth veered toward the pool entrance.

It was humid in here. The ceiling was twice as high as the diving board, and the place looked like it belonged in a movie, not a high school. The pool was Olympic-sized, and there were thirty students in the water, and all the instructors were sitting on the edge, seemingly ready to jump in at any time. The instructors were narrating and miming the action of diving. From just the minute Garth observed them, if the students didn't already know how to dive, that was too bad for them. They were probably graded separately.

He walked along the edge, keeping as far away from the chlorine water as possible. Garth recognized Sasha at the other end of the pool, the deep end. He approached. Sasha noticed him from the corner of her eye and stood up to meet him.

"Mister Hood. Long time no see."

"Ms. Grace. I wanted to ask you something. You free for a minute?"

"Sure." She turned to the students. "Everybody, keep practicing. I'll be back." She turned back to Garth.

They walked a few paces away from the pool and stood by the wall.

"What did you need?"

"Actually I don't need anything. I just wanted to see what you do all day."

Sasha laughed and gestured to the pool. "This is my office. One more period and it's math time."

"I've never seen the school's pool until now. Wow. So this is what the school blew its whole budget on."

"All this to compete in the state swimming competitions."

"I was surprised when I saw the weight room, how nice it is. Still doesn't make sense. They'll blow their money on stuff like this, but they won't hire new teachers to reduce class size."

"It makes perfect sense, Mister Hood. You know it."

"I know. It's just like the vending machines. Don't do anything that won't make you money."

"So how are the pups doing? Gonna put some muscle on them?"

"I'm trying. I think all the serious ones are on the teams. I'd like to see some gains. We'll find out when the numbers from the nurse start changing."

"Those numbers will determine if you have a job next year. Remember that."

"I know. Seems a bit excessive though, weighing the students to track gains. So far nobody's been injured, and they really do seem to respect me. Except in Government. I feel like such a fake. I'm just reading the book to them. Everything I say and do is scripted."

"Everyone does. I feel like one all day in here."

"Every day I wish I could do something else, something that will really engage those pups. Something besides reading the book to them. I did assign a book report. Hopefully that will help."

"Don't let it get to you. It's just a job. You're not here to change the world. Just do what they ask, collect your money and go home."

"I may as well do a good job while I'm here. If they see I'm willing, maybe they'll promote me."

Sasha smiled, and then looked away. "I'll catch up to you later, Garth. I have to go. Bye."

"Thanks for your help," Garth said, loud enough to echo.

Sasha rejoined the pups at the pool. Garth walked on, through the showers and into his office. He closed the door behind him and smelled dobie again. Garth spun around. Evan was standing there wearing nothing but his gym shorts, limp cock outlined blatantly against his thigh. His backpack was on the floor, open, a small bottle visible inside.

"Evan!" Garth said.

The doberman grinned, pulled down his shorts and kicked them off. He grabbed himself and turned it around a few times, clockwise, counterclockwise, and then let it dangle.

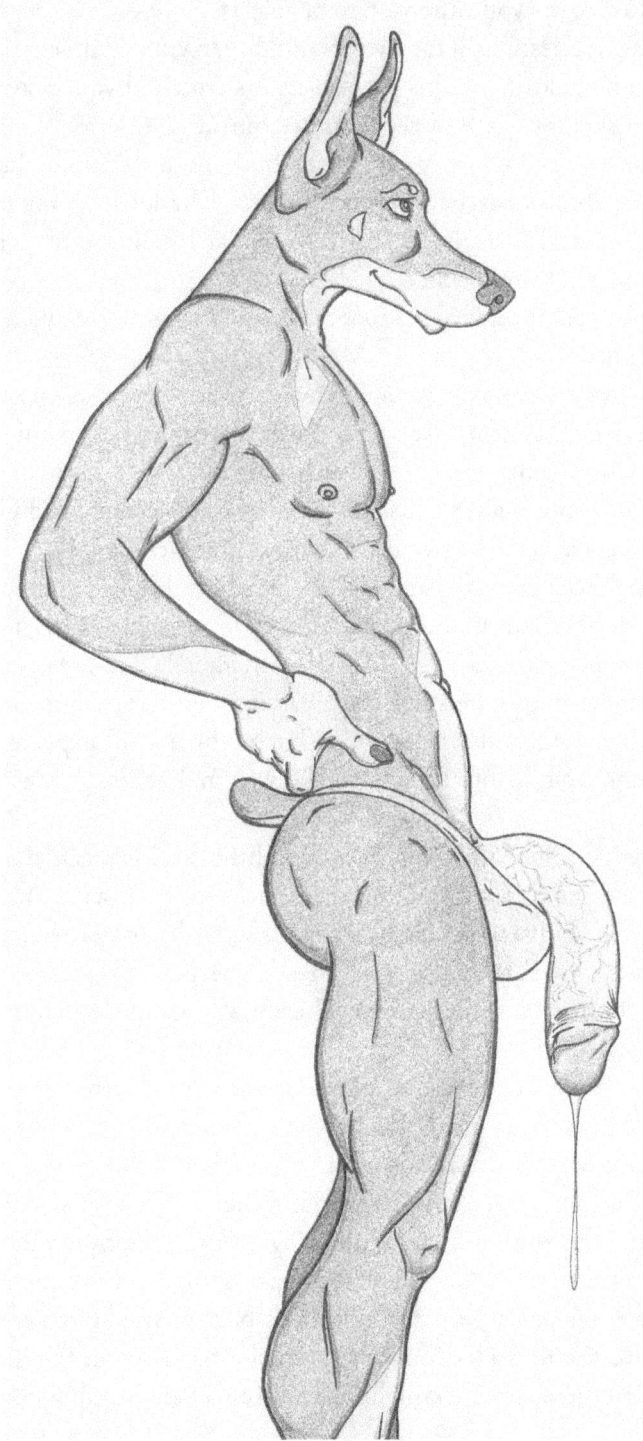

"Evan, aren't you supposed to be in class?"

"Lunch doesn't end for twenty minutes, plenty of time."

Garth couldn't take his eyes off Evan's crotch. "Evan, okay, that's the hottest thing I've ever seen, but we can't..."

Evan reached down, grabbed the bottle, squirted some lube on his fingertip and reached behind himself. The look on his face—pure greed and lust aimed squarely at Garth—was catchy. Evan's cock jumped at the touch.

"I can smell you want it, too. Sit down. I want to ride you."

"Evan..."

"No one knows where I am. Monitors didn't even see me leave."

He straightened up, walked towards Garth and began pulling up his shirt, licking his lips. Garth wanted to pull it back down, but then Evan's cock rose higher, brushed against Garth's crotch, and Garth's defenses collapsed. Evan pulled the mastiff's shirt off.

Evan drooled at the sight of Garth's chest. He felt the mastiff's pecs with both hands and pushed Garth into the chair. Evan undid Garth's pants and slid them down. Garth already had pre on the tip and Evan used his lubed paw to spread it around. He climbed up on the chair, aimed, and sat down on Garth. The mastiff expected it to take some time before he was all the way in, but Evan went down easily.

Garth grunted and panted through his nose. He reached behind Evan, held his rear with one paw and held his back with the other. Evan braced himself on Garth's biceps as sat up halfway, then lowered all the way down. Evan's cock was nestled between Garth's pecs, and with each thrust it rose up to meet his muzzle. Garth leaned forward and licked the tip.

Evan moaned as more blood rushed to Garth's groin and thickened his meat inside Evan. The dobie smiled at Garth, lifted up and sat back down. He opened his mouth as if moaning but kept silent. Garth wrapped his paws around the pup's length and rubbed it while Evan rode him slowly, feeling every separation and valley between his muscles. Garth had to suppress his own voice constantly.

Evan tightened his grip on Garth's biceps, lifted himself up to the tip of the mastiff's cock and then slid back down. He did this three times in a row, fucking himself harder than Garth would have believed he could take. Garth held Evan's back in one hand and his dick in the other, rubbing it up and down as Evan squeezed Garth's arms.

He speared himself several times like this. Garth wanted to thrust, but the chair was too flimsy. Then he paused with Garth all the way inside him. He was looking in Garth's eyes, and Garth returned his contented gaze. The mastiff leaned forward and spoke into Evan's ear through gritted teeth.

"My God, pup, you're good!"

Evan licked his lips, and then licked Garth's. "I know. And so are you. I don't think I can hold it."

"Already?"

"You're so hot I could cum just looking at you."

He was still holding Garth's arms as he pulled himself up and sat back down, taking Garth to the hilt. Garth growled, licked the pup on the muzzle.

Evan turned his muzzle up and rode Garth harder and faster. His muzzle was open, and he obviously wanted to scream and holding it all in was painful. Not moaning or screaming took enormous effort for Garth as well. Gritting his teeth wasn't helping anymore. Garth guided Evan's tip up to his muzzle and suckled on it. Evan looked like he was about to lose it.

Evan was riding Garth so fast he had pushed the chair against the wall. Garth couldn't stop himself from thrusting, and the chair squeaked. Garth's paws wandered around to Evan's rear and cupped it. He lifted Evan up and allowed the pup to slide back down. Again Garth lifted him more than halfway up his shaft, and then Evan slid back down. It was like lifting weights, and it made Garth's arms huge. Evan noticed, and set the pace faster and faster, feeling Garth's muscles in motion.

Garth felt hot liquid on his tongue. The Doberman's cum tasted better every time, and he squeezed every drop he could out of Evan with both paws. Evan had never let go of Garth's arms. The dobie was still feeling them, even as he went soft and dripped cum on Garth's chest.

Evan smiled. Garth growled, reached under Evan's arms, lifted him up and set him on the floor. Evan took the hint and kept his legs raised. Growling and panting, Garth pounded Evan as deep and as fast as Evan had when the dobie was in control. Evan kept smiling, feeling Garth's arms all the way around. Garth was impressed Evan was able to handle this so well, and he growled as he buried himself deep in the pup, drooling on him.

Evan wrapped his arms around Garth's back as the mastiff growled deeper and thrust into the pup harder and harder. Evan threw his head back, raising his legs higher, trying to give Garth more room to go even deeper. Evan's paws wandered to his triceps and he braced himself on those.

Garth's dick rammed Evan's hot ass a few more times, and then he pushed his muzzle against Evan's flat chest and moaned. Evan's cock rested right beside his nose. It was hard again and leaking pre. The sight of it made Garth even harder and he felt climax rushing up from his hips.

He muffled his growling against Evan's chest, and then blew his load deep in Evan. It lasted even longer than last time. Garth had never cum this much before, and it was like his dick pulsed for a solid minute before it finally calmed down.

Garth pulled out of Evan. The dobie lowered his legs and looked at Garth, panting. "Wow, Garth. That was... You are..." All he did was smile.

Garth couldn't say anything either. Now they heard the sound of the showers running. Pool class was letting out. Garth and Evan looked at each other, thinking the same thing.

They stood up, dressed only in shorts, and slipped into the shower area together. They found separate stalls, cleaned off, stood in the dryers and dressed up again. Evan made a stop at the bathroom just off to the side of the showers.

Garth was sure the whole school knew, but the bell rang, Garth changed into his teacher clothes and went to Government Studies. He stood before the desk and read the text with more gusto than usual.

At the end of the first Government period, Garth resolved to stay away from the pup. Somehow, he had to.

Chapter 10

"Oh, thanks for stopping by, Mister Hood," said the poodle behind the desk.

Garth stepped inside and stood next to one of the chairs. "Did you need me?"

"Yes, I wanted to ask you how Student Council is doing."

"We've only had one meeting, but I guess it's all right."

"You are reading your scripts?"

Garth hesitated, stared. "What would happen if I said no?"

"Then I would have to strongly suggest you begin, as they are very important."

"To who?"

"To the school, Mister Hood."

"Ms. Dover, please tell me the school district has made you a sock puppet and you don't really believe in any of this stuff."

"It's my job to believe in what I'm doing, just like you."

"I'm not paid enough to believe in what I'm doing. Not yet. Are you?"

"Pay is confidential, Mister Hood."

"I know."

"Anyway, now that you have experience guiding those students, I think you're ready to help the school in other ways."

"What now?"

She handed him a paper. Garth took it and read the header.

"Now you want me to run the speech team?!"

"You won't be running it, Mister Hood. Mrs. Sinclair runs it. You will be her assistant. It's even easier than Student Council. All you have to do is find props for the students, anything the lessons require. Anything Mrs. Sinclair requires."

Garth was skimming the paper. He felt the fur standing up.

"Twice a week," Ms. Dover continued. "Will twice a week be a problem?"

"Yes, it will. I'm already out of the weight room once a week. This will leave me two days a week in the weight room to make sure those pups stay on the routine the school wants me to put them on."

"Mister Hood, I have heard of your excellent job getting those children on a workout plan, and I commend you for it. But the children know their routines by now. You don't have to be there all the time anymore. It is important that we utilize our time wisely."

"You trust the pups to do their routines perfectly because you haven't met any of them. They try to take risks all the time. They want to play games on the weights. They want to compete with each other. I have stopped so many of them from doing stupid things that could land them in the hospital. I need to be there."

"They have their routines, and you have corrected them for a whole week. You need to make the most of your time. Speech meets Tuesdays and Thursdays. You're only an assistant."

"May I get an assistant?"

"You have other coaches who can cover you in the weight room while you're gone."

"If any of those pups hurts himself, you'll blame me, but I'll be out of the room doing errands for Student Council or speech team or something, and my coverage will probably be hiding in his office playing Angry Foxes on his phone."

"Mister Hood, I get the feeling you are not very open to change."

"You hired me to get the wrestling and football teams lifting weights. Do you want me to do my job?"

"Always."

"Then stop putting things on me that are not my job."

"This comes from the board of directors, Mister Hood. It's not going to change. We have to work within the system we are given."

"Right," Garth turned around.

"I have faith in you, Mister Hood. I know you can do this."

Garth growled on his way out, hoping she didn't hear him. He walked down the empty hallway and turned into the gymnasium, wondering whose idea it was to give out new assignments on Fridays.

It just left the employees pissed off all weekend. Perhaps it was a new management trend sweeping the country.

Garth sat down on the bleachers, holding the paper. He smelled mastiff scent standing over him, and Garth looked up at Terrance.

"What's new?" said the dog.

"I'm now the assistant to speech team."

"Mrs. Sinclair needs more than an assistant." Terrance sat down next to him, his fat taking half a second to settle after his rear was on the seat. "How's your acting?"

"Never done it, I'm a physicist. Doesn't Joey need an assistant?"

"Yeah, but they won't give him one."

"Terrance, this means I'll be out of the weight room three days a week. Someone needs to be in there to watch these pups. The ones in gym unit don't worry me. They don't want to work out, but the ones on the wrestling and football teams? They think they can do anything and there will be no consequences. I don't want someone to screw up his back on my watch."

"I knew this was gonna happen, Garth. We'll keep an eye on them."

"At this rate I won't be in the gym at all."

"It's the way this place is."

Garth sighed. First bell rang in five minutes, so it was time to put emotions away and be teacher. When all the pups and kits arrived, the coaches took attendance, and Terrance declared another free day. The students picked up basketballs and started dribbling. Garth wondered if these pups knew how to do anything besides dribble a basketball.

It was not professional to be seen sitting around doing nothing, so he took his paper and retreated to his office. He paused at the door, sniffed the air inside. He did not smell doberman, and he was relieved. He walked inside, closed the door and sat down in the chair, leaned on the desk and took a few deep breaths.

He was sure he didn't need to be in the room all the time. Absent once a week was reasonable, but three times a week was too much. He glanced at the clock. He had almost an hour. He picked up the paper, walked through the lockers and left through the pool. Sasha was sitting on the side of the pool, instructing students. Other coaches were at the shallow end, working with the pups who were not good swimmers.

The shepherd/collie saw him from a distance and waved. Garth waved back and exited through the side door directly into the hallway. He crossed the halls, followed the numbers and found Mrs. Sinclair's room. He knocked on the door.

A moment later, a large canine opened the door. "Yes?"

"Sorry to bother you, Mrs. Sinclair?" Garth said.

She nodded.

"I'm Garth Hood. Ms. Dover said I'm your new assistant in..."

Garth just noticed why she was large. She was very pregnant.

"She told you assistant?" Mrs. Sinclair said.

"Yeah. That's what she said."

She turned around and addressed the classroom, "Just a moment." She stepped out of the room and closed the door behind her. "Mister Hood, I'm glad you'll be here. I'm due in less than a month. I told them I needed someone else trained to take this job while I'm on leave. They ignored me right up until the last minute, and now we have a week or three to prepare you to run it."

Garth growled and his fur rose. Mrs. Sinclair winced.

"I'm not mad at you. I'm mad at *her*."

"Lilith," she nodded. "I told them last year this was coming, and what did they do? They dragged their feet. They tell us to solve problems before they become a problem, and then they do this. I'm sorry you got stuck with this, Mister Hood. Do you perchance have any acting experience?"

"None."

"Well, you'll get some next week. I'll give you one of the textbooks so you can get an idea of where we are and where we're going. One minute."

She opened the door and slipped back inside. The pups were murmuring amongst themselves. Garth stood still and waited patiently, and then he peered through the glass panel and recognized a few of the pups from the football and wrestling teams. He shook his head, opened the door the rest of the way and stepped inside.

"Coach Hood!" a few of them chorused.

Garth held up a paw and pointed at them, smiling. "Don't call me coach."

One of them shoved another pup in the shoulder, "Told you he was huge."

"This pup didn't believe us when we told him you should be a pro!"

"Show him your biceps!" said someone else.

Garth smiled and stood still. He figured just standing here in his gym clothes was enough.

Right about then, Mrs. Sinclair walked up to him and handed him a textbook with bookmarks in several places.

"I marked all the chapters we're going to cover in the next two weeks. Look over them so you'll know what to expect. I'll have more for you next week."

"Thanks. See you Tuesday."

"Thank you, Mister Hood."

"Bye, everyone," Garth said, waving to them, knowing full well it made his arm look huge.

The pups cheered as Garth left the room, becoming muffled when the door latched. Garth stepped away from the window in the door and smiled to himself. He looked at the book in his paws and read the cover. It was a theater textbook. He sighed and walked back to his office.

The weight of the task dumped on him was tremendous, and he wanted to hide in his office for the rest of the day. He hid in it the first period, reading the textbook, trying to figure out what he was supposed to do. When the bell rang, he picked himself up and remained in the open for the next four periods, watching the pups who were working out. Most had learned what not to do by now, so Garth wasn't worried.

Government Studies came and went. Evan seemed like a perfectly normal Doberman all of a sudden. Garth hoped it would last forever. During the period's downtime, Garth wondered if he could find a way to meet the pup over the weekend. It occurred to him all he had to do was ask, and he was sure it would happen. He shook the thought out of his head.

When class dismissed, Garth expected Evan to ambush him. During the last free day in gym, he looked over his shoulder a few times, wondering where Evan was and why he wasn't talking to him. Instead, Evan was playing basketball with three other dogs. Garth observed them for a while, and he noticed all of those pups were twice Evan's size. They really were the jocks of the school, and Evan should not be there. They seemed to treat Evan as an equal.

Garth smiled. He wanted to go in closer and hear what they were talking about, but he was glad they occupied Evan's attention. Maybe Evan would forget about Garth entirely and focus on them.

School ended, and A-shift workouts began. Garth made it a point to stay in the weight room and supervise all the pups and kits who were working out. One of the jocks Garth saw Evan playing basketball with was on bench press with no spotter. Garth walked through the room, stood over the rack and spotted the weights for him.

"I'm sorry, what's your name again?" Garth said.

The white-furred canine benched ninety, which was pretty good for someone his age just starting out. His form was good, but he was going too fast.

"Cas."

"Cas?" Garth said.

"Short for Casper."

"Listen, slow down, you're going too fast. If you want gains, do slow reps."

Cas listened to him and halved his speed.

"That's better. Keep that pace." Cas did a few more reps. Garth took a deep breath. "I wanted to ask you something."

"What?"

"That doberman you were playing basketball with last period. Evan Silvers."

Cas smiled. "What about him?"

"He seemed very out of place among that group. Three jocks and Evan?"

He was still smiling. "What do you wanna know?"

"Why do you let him hang around you?"

He had done ten reps, and Garth helped him set the bar back on the rack. Cas still lay on the bench, staring up at Garth upside down. "Don't let him fool you. He's tiny, but he fits right in."

"Good at basketball?"

"And a lot more."

Garth wanted to ask directly, but he remembered what Sasha told him. He shouldn't trust teachers, or students.

"He still looks like he doesn't belong."

"I thought so, too, but he convinced us."

He raised his arms. Garth helped him lift the barbell and position it where it should be. Garth corrected his form, observed the others from a distance. Everyone else was doing well. No games, no posturing, no trying to impress friends. All was well so far, and he was glad Evan wasn't in the gym today.

Chapter 11

The weekend had been endless anticipation and preparation for the following week. He read a few chapters in the theater textbook, and a few chapters ahead in the Government textbook, trying to come up with other things to do in class besides read the chapters to the students. He came up with nothing else. If he'd had time to prepare a course, he might have been able to, but between the speech team and everything else, Garth just didn't have the time.

Now, Tuesday night, Garth stood in Mrs. Sinclair's classroom facing the students on speech team. He watched her, observed what she did and how she guided the students. Speech team was all about performance, monologues and famous speeches in literature, theater, film, and real life. The students were doing an exercise on acting, and some of them had not quite coordinated hand gestures with spoken words, so they would say a few lines, then move their hands, then say another line, move their hands again.

After two hours of observation, Garth stood up from the desk as the students left for the busses. Mrs. Sinclair turned to him.

"What did you think?"

"I understand what you're doing, but I don't know how you intend to get them from where they are to where they should be."

"Practice, Garth, lots of practice. Some of these students were on the team last year, so they already know. The others, well mostly you give them a scenario, or a script, and tell them to act it this way. Then act it that way. Then you give them feedback as an observer."

Garth shook his head. "They want me to do this? I'm a physics major. I'm not an actor."

"They'll do all the work. All you have to do is guide."

"Sure. What if they want to see me to perform?"

She smiled. "Would you like some acting lessons?"

"Right now?"

"We have time for one."

"Well, sure," Garth said, smiling. "What can I do?"

Mrs. Sinclair grinned. "Here's an easy one. Pretend you are drowning."

Garth blinked.

"Right where you stand, your head it below water and you're struggling for air struggling trying to climb the water—" and she was doing it, "—you can see the light above and you can't breathe!"

Garth copied her gesticulating, held his breath, tried to put himself in the frame of mind. Mrs. Sinclair stopped, letting Garth take over.

"Eyes bigger! You're panicking! Every muscle in your body wants to take a breath, and you're fighting it, you're fighting it!"

Garth felt silly standing here waving his arms around. He wasn't feeling it at all, and slowed to a stop, giggling and shaking his head.

"They want me to take over?" Garth said. "There must be someone better."

"Acting is empathy, Garth," she said. "Some of the best actors in the world are also the most empathetic people you could ever meet. They can imagine how someone feels in any given circumstance, and become that emotion, letting that feeling take over."

"Well what about celebrities? They don't seem very empathetic."

"They would be if the paparazzi left them alone."

"Yeah, point. So how'd I do?"

"Practice, Garth. Everyone feels silly at first. We'll try again Thursday."

"Bye, Mrs. Sinclair."

He walked out of the classroom and down the hall. Garth paused. He looked over his shoulder at the empty hallway. He tried to lower his fur and then walked onward.

He passed through the empty gym and into the lockers. He heard the water running again. He ignored it at first, but then he heard claw clicks against the tiles. Garth walked to the second to last stall and stopped. The water was running, but no one was in there. He shook his head, began to turn the other way when an arm wrapped around his neck from behind.

"Surprise!" Evan's giggly voice said.

The arm pulled him into one of the empty shower stalls. Evan was against the tile wall, holding Garth against him, hard cock between his cheeks.

"I dreamed about you all weekend," Evan said, voice becoming sultry all of a sudden. His arm lowered from Garth's neck to his

chest, and wandered around his stomach. One found his crotch. "Oh, I see you're in the mood, too."

Garth stepped away from him, easily breaking his grip. "Evan..." he turned around. Evan was completely naked, and at full mast. Garth had forgotten just how big it was and he froze up again. Evan leaned against the wall, arms behind his head, smiling ear to ear.

"This is getting too dangerous," Garth said. "We need to break this off, now."

Evan reached under Garth's shirt and felt his abs. One paw wandered below the waist and began to undo his pants. Garth backed away. Evan stepped forward to match him. Now Garth was against the tile wall.

Evan pulled Garth's pants down all the way. Evan licked his lips at the sight of it, and he dropped to his knees and immediately started nursing the dog's throbbing shaft. Garth pressed himself against the wall and panted. The more he felt the pup's muzzle, the more he realized how much he wanted to pound that ass again.

Evan came up for air, looked up at Garth. "I really wanna fuck you. You ready for me?"

"Hell, no! I'd need a couple hours to make that thing fit!"

"I can give you that," Evan said, licking his lips again.

Garth looked down at him. Evan smiled at him, and with both hands under Garth's shirt, he rose to his feet, hands traveling up Garth's abs and over his chest. He rubbed Garth's chest muscles all around, licking his lips, grinding his crotch against Garth's.

Garth growled, unbuttoned his shirt and threw it off, seized the pup and slammed him onto the tile, practically lying on Evan. The smaller dog smiled, licked Garth's muzzle and wrapped his arms around his back.

The mastiff just now noticed Evan's backpack in the corner of the stall, zipper open, and a bottle of lube prominently poking out. Garth snatched it, lubed himself up, stood up and positioned himself over Evan. The dobie looked surprised Garth was actually going to do it, and he held it steady.

Garth sat down, the tip poking his hole and spreading him out. Garth grunted and panted as he lowered himself past the head and began working on the shaft. He kept himself loose just in case he ever met somebody, but he never expected to meet somebody like this. It was much thicker than any of the toys he had.

Garth rose and sat back down, taking another half inch. He gritted his teeth and kept his muzzle shut, hoping that would muffle any sound. He rose another inch, then took another half inch, howling through his teeth again.

Evan had both hands on his cock, holding it steady for Garth, licking his lips at the sight of Garth's muscles moving under stress again. The strain of taking a rod this size had pumped him up so much his veins were visible all across his torso and arms, even through the fur. Evan was wide-eyed and rock hard drinking it in.

Garth sat up, went down, pushing his limit more and more each time. The veins on his arm were enormous and thick. Evan was feeling them with one paw, still holding his cock still with the other. Garth felt precum squirting into him. Evan moved from the arm to one of his pecs, tracing the veins there, too. Veins Garth didn't know could be visible.

Garth went down several more times, but he wasn't making any progress. It was in as far as it would go. The whole thing did not fit, and he could not sit all the way down on Evan, but all the important parts did, and he considered it victory. Garth raised himself and sat back down until he felt strain. Evan's paws were now free to roam across Garth's thighs as the mastiff did squats on Evan's cock, slowly, at the proper pace. Evan's eyes were wide and enraptured by the sight of all that muscle moving.

Garth tried to match the pace Evan had fucked himself on Garth, but it was too thick to ride that fast. He was content with this, and Evan seemed content with Garth's pace as well.

Evan couldn't get enough of Garth's thighs at work. As he watched he began to thrust Garth, pushing the dog's limit even more. After a few of these, Garth took the hint and held still as Evan bucked his hips, as if trying to throw Garth off.

The dobie held Garth's thighs and thrust faster and harder. Garth leaned over, hands on either side of Evan's head and met Evan's eyes. Evan was swimming in ecstasy. Moments later, Evan held still and moaned. Garth felt Evan's dick pulsing and seed filling him up. He relished the feeling. He had been filled many times before, but that was the first time he saw a cock he wanted to fill him up until he burst.

Evan was obviously spent, but Garth growled, stood up and liberated himself from Evan's rod and lay down on the pup, pinning him in place. Evan panted, smiling ear to ear, arms wrapping around Garth's rear, fingering his used hole.

Garth growled deeper, adjusted his hips and held his tip against Evan's hole. The dobie raised both legs, and Garth pushed in all the way to the hilt. Garth knew the pup could take it, so he was not

gentle or gradual about it. Evan still held him, the look on his face telling him he was spent but he wanted to keep going. Garth pulled out halfway and shoved himself back all the way in. Evan's paws wandered up Garth's back and he braced himself on him as Garth buried his cock in him again and again.

Garth had already been nearly at the point of finishing before he even entered the younger dog, and had taken real effort not to finish as soon he was in him. Garth kept his pace slower than his body wanted to go. Evan licked Garth's muzzle, held onto his triceps, smacking them from time to time, feeling how solid they were.

Garth knew how to keep himself from finishing now.

"Tell me," Garth said. "What did you do to Cas?"

"What do you mean?"

"To make all those jocks respect you. What did you do? Why do they let a pup half their size play basketball with them?"

Evan smiled. He was getting hard again. Garth could feel it growing up his stomach. When it touched his chest, Garth somehow got harder, making Evan moan and pant.

"Couple years ago, Cas was picking on me. He thought he could push me around. He was on football team even then, so during practice I snuck into the locker room. Nursed a hard on for half an hour so I was nice and slick. I heard them coming back and I hid in the corner. Pulled him back, turned him around and started licking his muzzle."

Garth started to thrust again. Evan's voice only wavered a little bit.

"I grind him. He looks down, sees it, and he doesn't run. Now all the other football players wondered where he was, 'cause they moved on. They find us in the corner, me kissing him, cock out, soaking his shirt with pre. All they did was walk away. They left me alone with him... ooooohhhh."

Garth was at it like an animal again. Evan held onto him tighter as Garth pounded him deep and hard.

"It's how they haze new players," Evan continued, more strained now. "They let them meet me. I did it to a bunch of 'em. Most aren't in this school anymore, but the dogs I was playing basketball with were. I hazed all of them. They don't pick on me anymore, and there aren't any bullies in this school."

"Thanks to you?"

Evan nodded. "They let me put 'em in their place."

"You like doing that, don't you?"

Evan smiled, hands moving from triceps to biceps. Garth plowed him fast and deep again.

"You don't mind missing the bus?" Garth said.

"I can walk. Oooooh, this is amazing!"

Evan was hard again, and leaking pre all over Garth's chest and stomach. Garth growled and Evan held on and tried not to scream as Garth stayed deep and rammed him fast. Garth growled and thrust him a few more times, then lay down on Evan and shoved it in one last time. Garth filled him up, looking into the pup's eyes as he did. Evan licked his muzzle. Garth licked his muzzle back. He was still cumming.

Garth spoke only when his dick finally stopped. "Evan, you're good. I mean that not as your teacher, but a gay dog who's been around the block a lot. But we can't keep doing this."

"What's your address?" Evan said. "I don't drive, but I have a bus pass."

"Whoa. No way. Anybody sees us together outside of school, they'll know something's wrong."

"Nothing is wrong," Evan said, reaching behind Garth's head, pulling him closer to lick his muzzle again.

"You bet your sweet ass this is. It's hot, but it's so wrong. I'm about old enough to be your father."

Evan smiled wider, reached up, felt Garth's cheek. "Daddy!"

"Nope."

Garth pulled out quickly. Evan gasped and panted, dropped his legs and lay still, tongue hanging out.

"Get dressed. We have to get out of here. Separately. You're a good fuck, Evan, I mean it, but this is the last time."

Garth pulled his pants up and buttoned them. Evan was still sprawled out on the floor, legs spread, chest fur still wet with Garth's pre. His dick was leaking pre again, and it reached his chest. Garth started to get hard again just looking at it. Evan licked his muzzle as he spoke.

"You keep saying that, and we always end up dirty."

"I know. If I lose this job for fucking around with you, I may never get another job in my field. You'll have a record, too. There's too much to lose."

"I've been doing stuff like this since middle school. Nobody cares."

"Here, maybe, but out there it's different. Go fuck around with those jocks. I can't do this anymore."

"I do fuck around with them. That's why I don't see you every day."

"Oh, God. Stay with them then."

"They're not as big as you. And not nearly as much fun! They don't fuck me as hard as I want them to!"

"Go home, Evan. This is the last time. I promise."

Garth walked away, leaving Evan sprawled out on the floor. He didn't even stop in the bathroom before going to his car. He drove home as fast as he could so there would be no chance of seeing the pup again.

At home, on the computer, while filling out a job application, Garth clenched his fists thinking how he had to let Evan go like that. In every possible way, life just was not fair.

Chapter 12

"Next topic up for discussion," Garth said, trying to make it look like he wasn't reading from a paper. "Whether the school should upgrade its computers."

Gina, the opinionated boxer, was the first to speak. She seemed to have something to say about everything, and it inspired others to take part in it. This week, however, all of their discussions had merely degenerated into arguments, and as a moderator, Garth wasn't sure what he was supposed to do.

He listened to the students on the council talk endlessly about how nice it would be not to use operating systems that were five years old. They remarked their phones had more computing power than most of the machines the school had, and just when it looked like the argument was about to settle into a consensus, Garth stood up and recited his speech.

"All of you have brought up good points. However, one thing you should consider is cost. There are over two-hundred computers in this school. How much would it cost the school to upgrade all of them?"

"The school can afford it!" said Gina.

Garth made an uncertain face. "If that was true, we'd have fewer coaches in this school and a lot more teachers."

He scanned the room, suddenly afraid of listening devices embedded in the walls with a direct line to the Principal, or worse, Ms. Dover.

"Well we can upgrade some of them at least," one of the canines in the back said. "We don't have to do all of them."

Garth sat down as the students began talking amongst themselves. Evan was quiet, and Garth was doing his best to keep his eyes above Evan's waist. The pup's dick outline was so obvious Garth didn't need any imagination, and it took an act of will to stay soft. Concentrating on the argument helped a lot.

The pup never broke eye contact, or that smile. Garth listened to the students explore the issue, and now with this new element added to the mix, the debate changed.

Garth agreed with the scripts on some points. Budget was always a factor, and young dogs and cats needed to learn how to account for it. Garth felt like he was watching them grow up little by little right in front of him, going from idealistic, opinionated teenagers to young adults with more balance to their views.

Then there were the other points that were just blatant political agenda. "Taking responsibility for oneself?" "Stock only what is most likely to sell?" Why didn't the scripts mention the school was effectively pushing the cost of the lunches on a minority, using lack of budget as an excuse, and then calling it encouraging the felines to take responsibility for themselves?

Or that the school had a contract with the soda and snack companies to stock their snacks and beverages, which was the only reason those vending machines had the unhealthy crap in them? It wasn't about providing what sold, it was all about whoever had the contract because the school shared in the profits. It was in the school's best interest to stock only what sold.

These were the real issues they needed to debate, and they would be healthy angles to approach the topics, but they were not in the script, so he didn't mention them. Was he allowed? There wasn't enough time to debate that deep, but Garth wished he could try.

Garth wondered who wrote this. Perhaps some rich politician who wanted to make sure impressionable students learned the truth as he or she saw it.

Today, the scripted points Garth introduced into the debate effectively killed any hope of the students reaching a decision besides the status quo. When this debate reached a stalemate, Garth moved on to the last issue: filling soda machines. It occupied more time than all the previous debates combined, and all Garth could do was pretend to be busy on the computer. Just like last week, the same two students—the two most motivated to be active in their school and make a difference—volunteered to give up two of their study halls for the job. Again, Garth wished he could tell them how the school was taking advantage of their youthful eagerness to save a buck.

Student Council was over at last, and the pups left as a group. Garth was grateful he didn't have to do anything. Evan closed the door and swaggered over to Garth's desk, making sure to wag his dick under this pants.

"Evan, no."

The dobie dropped his backpack and squeezed himself through his pants, first with one hand, then with both. He licked his muzzle. Garth stood up, did not take his things with him and walked past Evan. Evan reached out with one paw and cupped Garth's crotch as he walked by.

"Got another story for you. Don't you want to hear it?"

Garth stood still, dobie's hand still on his bulge. "No. Go home."

"You're getting harder." Evan rubbed it and grinned, looking up at Garth's muzzle. "You want to do all sorts of things to me, don't you? I'd like to hear about them."

Evan rubbed faster and faster. Garth's crotch bulge was now obscene. Garth hopped away from the paw and looked Evan in the eye.

"We got lucky those last few times. No more."

Evan slipped his paws in his pockets and stood with his back arched, pushing his crotch out before him. "The school won't do anything about it. They never have before."

"They fired the last dog."

"I get away with it all the time."

"I'm not you, and the school doesn't need me. They can get rid of me any time and replace me with somebody else."

Evan shook his hips. His third leg bounced against his left thigh.

"Goodnight, Evan."

Garth walked past him, opened the door and walked out. He walked as fast as possible to his office, grabbed his things, and was out the door as soon as he could be. As he drove home, he thought about what he had said. He repeated it to himself several times on the road.

"The school doesn't need me. They can get rid of me. They can get rid of me..."

He wasn't sure why he had said that.

Chapter 13

"Mister Hood, how are things going?"

Garth was beginning to think Ms. Dover was not a real canine, but a robot bolted to the chair behind this desk. He wondered if he would find any legs if he peeked beneath the desk. Perhaps they shut her off every night. Garth imagined her torso halfway hung over the desk, plugged into the wall so she could recharge overnight and resume her automated duties of pushing random pieces of paper at carefully-selected canines.

Garth was skimming the piece of paper she had just pushed to him. His eyes caught keywords like lacrosse, assistant coach, and Terrance.

"Student Council not as bad as you expected?"

Garth skimmed on and saw that practice was on Monday, Wednesday and Thursday. He looked over the paper squarely at the poodle's muzzle.

"I already have Student Council on Wednesdays."

"You've observed them a couple times. Do they need both hours to come to an agreement on the points?"

"Yes."

"As moderator, you can encourage them to expedite the process."

"Am I allowed to tell them why?"

"Of course. Why wouldn't you be?"

The fur on Garth's back rose just a little.

"Mister Hood, the school hired you for a decent wage. We have to make sure you are earning it."

"And now the rest of my week is full. When am I supposed to be in the gym?"

"They have been fine without you so far."

"On Tuesday I had to stop someone from proving he could do four-hundred pounds on the incline rack. Good thing I was there or he would have ended up in the hospital. These are puppies and kittens. They have no idea how dangerous this is."

"The other coaches can handle keeping them safe. We need you elsewhere."

"Speaking of handling, why didn't you tell me Mrs. Sinclair was pregnant?"

"How was that relevant?"

"It means you didn't want me to be her assistant. You want me to take over for as long as she's on leave."

"Which I'm sure you can handle. The students know what to do. You'll just be there, giving them the exercises to do. It's all in the course outline and in the textbook. As in Government Studies, just follow those and you'll be fine."

"That's not what she does. She performs with them. She gives them tips on how they can be better. I know nothing."

"I have faith in you, Mister Hood. You can get this done."

Garth stood up, sliding the chair back. "Goodbye."

"Enjoy your day, Mister Hood."

He walked out and down the hall, growling to himself.

All Garth wanted to do was hide in his office, but instead he walked to the weight room and supervised the students as they did their little routines and filled out the papers. The whole time he thought about how he was going to be assistant coach of the lacrosse teams. Garth wasn't a religious person, but as the bell rang and it was time for his lunch period, he said a little prayer for all those students.

During his lunch break, Garth wandered the halls to clear his mind. His lunch was in the refrigerator in the lounge, but he didn't want to go there, so he kept wandering. Garth turned a corner, and something thin but surprisingly solid slammed into him from behind.

"Gotya!" Evan said. His voice echoed around the empty hallway.

Garth was off balance. The pup had him in a tight embrace and his legs were off the floor. Garth adjusted his stance and held Evan up easily. A paw wandered down to Garth's groin. Garth separated

Evan's hands and let him go. He dropped to his knees, looking up at him. Evan licked his lips.

"Evan..."

"Wanna see me suck myself?" He reached into his pants.

Garth turned around and walked away. He heard claw clicks on the floor catching up to him. Garth was tempted to speed up, but he was sure the pup could outrun him, so Garth set the pace and Evan walked beside him.

"Saw you wandering around. Thought I'd say hi."

"Go to lunch, Evan."

"I'd rather eat with you. I wanted to ask you something."

"Ask me during class, please."

"Is this where you want to be?"

Garth stopped, looked the pup in the eye. Evan's eyes were on Garth's, not his biceps.

"What do you mean?"

"I mean you could be out there winning competitions and stuff. I've seen dogs in magazines who weren't as big as you."

"Size isn't the only thing that wins."

"If you don't want to compete, why are you here?"

That lustful smile had dropped from Evan's muzzle. All of a sudden Garth felt comfortable around him, but he did not drop his guard in case another crotch-grab was coming.

"All right, I enjoyed working out and I kept going. When I was in college I found it great to do something physical, since my major was everything but."

"What did you major in? Nutritional Science?"

Garth chuckled. "Would you believe physics?"

Evan laughed and choked on it. "Seriously? You're a physics major?"

"PhD."

Evan's eyes were wide. "And you're here?"

"Teaching Government Studies and gym class, and soon to be coaching lacrosse and speech team. Welcome to real life."

"Oh... Wow."

"Get to lunch, Evan. I need to eat, too."

"You want my cell? I'd love to ask you some stuff."

"It wouldn't be appropriate, Evan. Please, just go to lunch."

Evan nodded, and then he reached out and grabbed Garth's crotch again. It caught Garth off guard because his face was not lustful. Garth leaped backwards a step and walked away, trying to make it look natural in case anyone saw.

Evan's claws clicked away in the other direction. Garth made a loop around the school and finally entered the teacher's lounge. He ate in there, alone, pondering how he was going to help Terrance coach lacrosse.

As Government Studies began, Garth realized he hadn't had a chance to look at the lessons. He really was reading from the book. While speaking the lines from the margin, Garth read further down at one of the suggested questions he was supposed to pose to the class. His words to Evan rotated in his mind. The school didn't need him. He was replaceable. Now that he had said it, he began to see it.

These notes were once used as a supplemental help for teachers. Now the innovation had been perverted into a means to replace teachers with low-paid gym coaches because all they had to do was read these notes to the students to make it appear they knew what they were talking about.

Anybody could do this, Garth thought during a pause for questions. *I am unnecessary. I am disposable. They don't want the best and the brightest. They want the worst because we're cheaper. How did this happen to our schools?* Later, as he sat behind his desk and watched the students work, he realized this is what his decade of education got him. A job so diluted by budget cuts anyone could do it. At this rate, his salary would pay off his loans by the time he retired.

Every action had an equal and opposite reaction.

He wondered if his employment agreement forbade him from telling them the truth about life outside the classroom. That one day, after they had followed their dreams in school and become the best of the best, the most they could hope for was a job in a corrupt school system reading from a textbook while secretly rushing students through the grades because he had to get his pups into weights so they could do better at sports.

Garth had the feeling these pups saw right through him. They had to. They must have seen through every teacher in the school and knew the whole thing was a sham.

By the second period of government studies, Garth realized it didn't matter what he said during class. Everything he could say was already in the book. All the school had to do was sit students down in the classroom, give them the book to read, and that would be the future of public schools. This may as well be a study hall.

The rest of the day was a blur. Fridays always were, since he had all day and all weekend to ponder his new task, and he had a feeling they would continue to be for the foreseeable future.

In the weight room after school, Garth stopped one feline from arching his back while doing bench. Garth saw it coming from across the room and shouted to the kitten to keep his back flat. He listened, and Garth was relieved. The students weren't playing around anymore, but they still made basic rookie mistakes. The school assumed they could wind the clock and walk away and it would run itself, but Garth would not want to risk it.

When the B-shift workout was up, Garth wandered back to the lockers. First he peeked around the corner, sniffed the air. He didn't smell doberman in here, so he walked to his office, paused at the door, scented the air inside, smelled it was empty and walked in.

As he walked through the school to the parking lot exit, he looked over his shoulder. No Evan. Garth breathed easier when he reached his car.

Chapter 14

Terrance stood beside Garth on the soccer field, which now had lacrosse nets on it. There were two teams, one for males and one for females. Nobody was in uniform, as those had not been ordered yet. The students merely loitered around the field. Garth expected them to be talking amongst themselves, but most of them were on their phones texting people. He wouldn't be surprised if some of those people they texted were standing right next to them.

"So they roped you into this, too?" said the overweight mastiff.

The muscular mastiff nodded.

"Yeah, she recruited me for the job, too," Terrance continued. "New lacrosse teams and they want me to keep up with basketball. They want more, but they won't hire new people to do it. I don't play lacrosse. If they want good players to compete with the other schools they should hire someone who knows the game. They want good coaching, don't make us do triple duty."

"I think that about a lot of things."

"Hell, Garth. Just give them drills and they'll get better. It's all we'll have time to do. School gets what it pays for."

"I should be in the weight room now," Garth said. "Is anybody watching those pups while I'm not there?"

"Sometimes."

Garth growled.

Terrance smacked Garth's wide back. "Lighten up. You're getting paid for this."

"I want to do a good job, not just get paid."

"You think I was always this fat? You think Paul was always a drunken wreak? Vern has another job on top of all this. Hasn't had a day off in two years. Pretty much just eats Raman. It's all he can afford, and his wife works, too. You think any of us wanted to end up here? If somebody else was hiring we'd all get the hell out of here."

Terrance walked away from Garth and took attendance. He and Garth divided the students into small groups, gave them lacrosse sticks and told everybody to practice tossing and catching the ball.

Garth had read the course outline for lacrosse Terrance was using to drill the students. Week one, perform these drills for this many days, then week two, these drills for so many days, give such-and-such lecture while the students practice.

Like every course in this school, everything was preplanned, every course pre-designed. They didn't need teachers to do this anymore. They could replace all teachers with interns who had no qualifications, and the results would be the same. Garth could see it happening right now, right before him. Schools were run like a business, and this was a natural step to take from a business perspective. While the world drilled it into students heads that school was essential to their future, business needs made sure those people were never hired.

Garth watched, wondering what he was supposed to do while the pups tossed the ball and tried to catch it. He couldn't offer advice, he couldn't coach, he couldn't lead. Neither could Terrance, and yet he shouted at many students to raise the arms higher, hold the stick right. Garth crouched and pretended to watch.

Evan wasn't in school today, and that bothered Garth. He looked over his shoulder from time to time, wondering if the pup was waiting for him in the bushes. After a while, Terrance walked up to him and looked down on Garth.

"I majored in anthropology," he said.

"Ms. Grace told me that."

"I wanted to be a professor. Even did some field work. Those people wanted to be there. They wanted to do that stuff. When I was in college, I imagined teaching would be like in the movies, with fiery debate and excited students."

Garth nodded, "Same here. These days nobody cares. They're there for the credit."

"They don't fucking care."

"Schools like this only make it worse."

"It's happening everywhere, and not just in the schools. This keeps up, every job will be like this. It's a paycheck. Come in, make the pups do stuff, kick back and figure out a way to grade them so everyone passes. Nice and easy."

"I could do so much more," said Garth. "I could give those students in government a real class. I could give the student council real debate. They're dumping so much on me I don't have time. Don't they want me to do a good job?"

"People who do a good job cost more. School doesn't want that, Garth. They want cheap teachers they can fire anytime they want. Yeah, they can fire us real easy now. If we don't follow the outline, they can terminate us. I came here willing to do a good job, and this is what they give me to work with. They blame us when the students don't win, you know. If this is all they want from me, it's all I'll give."

"It's not how it should be. We should be challenging these pups, preparing them for being out in the world."

"There's a college course for that."

"Why not just make high school part of college?"

"Someone's probably working on that."

Garth shuddered. He didn't want to believe it. Watching the students practice stick handling in lacrosse was boring and the time dragged on and on.

Tuesday was harsh. Garth felt so defeated and useless he didn't even keep up the image of teaching Government Studies. For his first period of it, he gave a quiz, declared it a study hall, ran to the grading machines by the copier, fed the test through one of them and received the students' scores instantly.

Garth hadn't smiled all day. He wasn't looking forward to speech team at all, and now he confirmed his Government class was the same whether he gave a lecture or not. It was all in the book, Garth's job was to read the book and do nothing outside of it. It was all the school wanted. He retrieved the papers and began walking down the hall back to his classroom.

He stopped about twenty paces from the door. Evan was leaning against the wall beside it, arms folded. At the sight of Garth, Evan's face lit up. He pushed away and walked up to him.

"Evan, what are you doing here?"

"Bathroom break. Wanna join me?"

"Go back to class."

"You don't mean that. I can tell. You're like all the other jocks, except you don't try to pick on me. One look at me and they totally deflate. Some of them swell up, trying to compete with me."

"See you next period."

Garth walked by him, expecting to feel a slap on his rear. None came, and Garth was relieved. He opened the door and walked inside. All his students were still here, still working. Only two had been on their phones, and they put them away as soon as Garth entered the room.

Garth was going to tell them not to pull a phone out in his class again, but he shook his head and sat down. What was the point of enforcing that? The class was a joke. Most of the students were finished with the next lesson anyway. It's not like they didn't have plenty of time.

Evan was well-behaved next period, though he still showed a little bulge. Garth coped by not giving a lecture again, and just played around on the computer. He wanted to search for jobs, but even now playing around on his phone would look bad.

The speech team meeting dragged on and on, and Garth watched and learned. Mrs. Sinclair decided this would be his last day to observe, and then he would try to take the helm while she sat at her desk and watched.

Mrs. Sinclair ran him through another acting lesson after the students dismissed. Garth was terrible at it, and Mrs. Sinclair was too polite to say so. As he walked to his car, Garth wished he had more time. He was sure he could do better if only he had more time to practice. Maternity leave was two months, which was a huge chunk of time out of the school year. Did the school want the speech team to succeed?

Garth walked back to his car, sat down and hung his head over the steering wheel.

On Wednesday, the gym coaches declared a free day, and Garth sat on the bleachers and watched dozens of students play basketball for four periods.

Government Studies became a study hall by default. Evan did not even look at Garth, and the physicist was glad.

Garth announced speech team would only be one hour on Thursdays when Mrs. Sinclair left for maternity leave because he was also coaching lacrosse. This wasn't welcome news. Garth understood why.

Garth hurried the Student Council through the various points on the list. There were so many points Garth could never do them all in just one hour, and for the ones he could do, pretty much all they had time to do was introduce the topic, have one or two opinions on the floor, and then Garth injected his speech and all debate stopped. Then the last half hour went to figuring out who would fill to soda machines next week.

As he watched the pups and kittens leave, he wondered if the Student Council was designed that way to make it easier on the disposable teacher they stuck with the task of moderating it. Don't challenge the students. Just make the class so easy it wouldn't even need a teacher.

Garth didn't have time to feel defeated because he had to change clothes quickly and go to the field. There he found Terrance running the students through the same drills as yesterday. Garth watched, and tried to give the impression he was following along.

When practice ended, Garth plodded across the field, looking down at his paws all the way to the school. Evan was waiting for him by his office door. He did not smile when he saw Garth.

"You okay, coach?"

Garth glared at him. The look of concern in Evan's eyes, the way he held his body, was absolutely unprovocative.

"Not today, Evan."

Garth walked past him, grabbed his things and walked out. The dobie did not follow.

On Thursday he only had to be there half the period of speech team, and then it was back to the lacrosse field. So much to do. So little time to do it. He wondered why he should bother trying to do a good job when the higher-ups clearly didn't want him to. They wanted an entire school full of low-paid, disposable teachers who didn't think, but were content to let the material they were given do the thinking. No challenge. Everybody passes, thinking they did well and were prepared for real life.

He took control of the coaching, and ran the students through the next drill on the list. He couldn't remember seeing Evan all day.

On Friday morning, about an hour before the school day began, Garth sat stone-faced in front of the desk, reading the paper Ms. Dover had just handed him.

"I'm sorry to do this to you, Garth."

Sure you are.

"We are opening a new advanced course on computer programming after school, and you have been chosen to helm it."

"An after-school course?"

"It's outside normal curriculum."

"And... you want me to teach it?"

"You'll mostly be a supervisor. The outline has all the materials and lessons you'll need."

"You really can't get someone who knows computer programming to do this?"

"There are no other qualified individuals at this school, at this time, Mister Hood."

"Can't the school hire someone?"

"We hired you. Now, this assignment will only be twice a week, and you have plenty of room on Tuesdays and Fridays."

Garth nodded.

"I have faith in you, Coach Hood. I know you can get this done, at this time."

"How long?"

"This course is a test run, so it will likely last until the end of the semester."

"All right."

"I'm glad you're being so cooperative. The school needs people like you, willing to bend and be multitalented."

"That's why I'm here."

Ms. Dover smiled professionally, thus ending the meeting. Garth rose from the chair and walked out, holding the paper at his side. He went to his office and set the paper on his desk, sat down and stared at it until it was time to show his face in the gymnasium.

He did so for attendance, and then retreated to his office for the rest of the period while the students enjoyed yet another free day. After school, Garth enjoyed his last day in the weight room with the football and wrestling teams. They were still making typical rookie mistakes, and they were more enthusiastic about building their bodies than he was.

Garth envied them. They didn't have to know how things around this damn school worked, and what would happen to them when they went to college and got a job in the real world. They could be happy texting on their phones and doing bench presses.

The physicist drove home and slept all weekend.

Chapter 15

According to the outline, the students should be proficient at catching and throwing by now, and it was time to start teaching coordination and teamwork. Garth and Terrance both agreed that was nonsense. It had only been one week, and half the players still couldn't catch. Everyone was good at throwing, but not aiming. The paper told them to move to the next phase of practice, so they moved on.

Garth blew his whistle from time to time.

So did Terrance.

Mostly they just watched from the sidelines as the students tried to do the drills the coaches had demonstrated. Garth and Terrance only picked up sticks once, but they never showed the students they couldn't catch or throw either. They always demonstrated sans ball, and it looked so professional, as if the coaches were so good at what they were teaching that a ball would only interfere.

After school on Tuesday, Garth welcomed the nineteen students to the extra-curricular computer programming course. Garth had not assigned seating, so the pups took seats at a terminal and eagerly waited to know what made this class so special they only offered it after school.

Garth had skimmed the first couple of lectures he was supposed to give and looked over the tasks he was supposed to assign the students. Garth had encountered program code many times in college, so he knew a few basics, but not enough to teach it.

He read the lecture, he read the book, and then gave an assignment. According to the outline, he was to occupy his time in a useful manner while the students performed the task. The book showed what the code should look like for the little program he told them to make, and in thirty minutes he was supposed to go around the room and check everybody's program to make sure it compiled and linked with no errors, behaved properly, produced the expected result, and that the code looked like what was in the book.

Every lesson was like this, a formula, a series of steps to duplicate day to day.

While Garth waited for his students to produce a program, he considered doing it with them, but he had a feeling he would not have time. Sure enough, one of the pups raised her hand and asked Garth a question. Fortunately, the educator's edition of the textbook had a list of likely questions students would ask, and this dog had asked number three. Garth gave the scripted answer, and the canine went back to work. Garth could only assume it was the correct response.

Garth wished he knew what he was talking about. He wanted to know this stuff, too. He wanted to learn with the students. A quiet voice in Garth's head said that maybe if he demonstrated he was a good worker and he was willing to go above and beyond to help these students and showed he had skill and talent for it, they would promote him to this department permanently and get rid of his extraneous jobs.

A new, louder voice reminded him that this school would not see it that way. They would only see that he was now willing to do *good* work for no extra pay, and they would thus heap more on him.

Instead, Garth walked around, answered questions as best as he could, and as the students raised their hands and announced they were done, Garth walked from student to student and examined their code and marked a box on their papers showing the exercise was complete and satisfactory.

The hour was up, class dismissed, and now it was time to break away and visit the speech team. When he arrived in Mrs. Sinclair's office, speech practice was well underway, and she was helping one of the new students become used to public speaking. Garth hoped he would be able to do so as well when it came time.

Wednesday's Student Council was pathetic. The students spent the entire time arguing over soda machine duty, and Garth sat and watched. He had so much to say, but he didn't see the point. Telling them wouldn't change anything coming down from the top.

Garth saw Sasha on Thursday between classes. They stopped in the hall, said hello, and stared at one another. Students walked around them, annoyed people had stopped in the middle of traffic.

Sasha seemed different. The consciousness seemed to have drained from her face, and now she was here merely in body. Garth was positive she saw the same thing on his face.

"Welcome to real life," Garth said.

"Yeah. Welcome. See you around, coach."

"Nice to see you again, Ms. Grace."

They parted.

Evan had become just another student, though Garth caught the pup following him several times. Now Evan kept his distance, and Garth was free to breathe easy at last. He even kept his cock outline hidden during Government Studies class.

The unit he was in right now was on various government structures around the world, how they worked, and what influence they had in their respective countries. He almost choked on one of the side notes in the margin, which wanted him to get the students involved in a discussion of the pros and cons of the various arrangements.

As if they would know what the pros and cons would be. Someone should be teaching them what the pros and cons are. Someone who knows.

All Garth could do was sit behind the desk and let the students read the book.

He realized he hadn't been in the gym for some time, not just in school, but outside of it. He didn't miss working out at all, and he wasn't sad to hear the weight unit of gym class was coming to an end.

On Friday morning, Garth once again sat in Ms. Dover's office. The poodle slid some papers Garth's way, and he took them.

"Now that the weight room unit is over, and you have some free time, I think this task is appropriate for you, Coach Hood."

The title page read: "Guide to Writing a Class Outline." He looked up at her.

"You want me to write an instruction guide for a weight room program?"

She nodded. "We could have used the outline already available to all schools in the district. I didn't give it to you at the start of the year because I wanted to see if you could come up with a better workout program for the athletes. From everything I have heard, you have done an outstanding job. We feel you could do a much better job at creating a new outline, exclusive to this school."

The quiet voice told Garth this was a great opportunity for career advancement. If he proved he could write a class outline that would open some doors for him in the future to do other courses. He could eventually get a university job with that kind of experience.

The louder voice told Garth that they were making him take part in his own depreciation, and that of all teachers, if not school itself. He was writing the guide they would later use to replace him with someone who would do the job for even less money, and they were not going to pay him for it.

"When does this need to be done?" he said.

"There's no hurry, but within the month if possible. Two months and I'll have to start prodding you." She smiled and laughed.

Garth smiled and imitated her laugher. "I'll start work on this soon."

"Thank you, Mister Hood. You're a valuable asset to this school."

That's not what this guide says.

Today was the last day of the weight unit, and Garth gave a little test, collected all the workout papers from the pups and kits in his unit and took them to the computer for grading. Everybody passed. The test was in the unit outline, and it was so easy a kindergartener would pass it. Passing students made him look good, and made the school look even better. Challenging them only risked someone failing, and his job was not to challenge anybody. The school had no budget for that.

The book report from Government Studies was due today, and Garth collected their papers. Garth was hoping to grade them today, but now he had a course on computer programming to teach after school. His lecture was extra long today, but by the end of it he thought he understood a little more as well. The students had a whole hour to work on the program he assigned them, but there were still questions. Questions Garth could answer only because he had read ahead in the book, and the students did not receive a textbook for this course. Everything was lecture and hands-on assignment.

Walking around, answering questions, and checking their programs occupied him the entire hour, and then it was finally time to go home.

After dinner, Garth was so tired he didn't even want to look at the book reports. At his computer desk, he picked off the one on top and began reading. This student had chosen a book by some political pundit who claimed the liberals were ruining the country. Another student selected a book that stated the conservatives were ruining the country. Each book gave all sorts of evidence, and the students repeated the evidence very well. Neither had given serious investigation to the other side.

Garth wished he could assign these students each other's book. He wished he could encourage them to look at both sides of the issues and think a little harder about them.

He had debated quantum mechanics with professors three times his age; he gave his thesis to a live audience made up of people who actually worked in the field; he stood up for himself when one of his professors told him he was wrong—but none of this prepared him to handle teenagers. If there was anything worse than dealing with people who were confident because they knew what they were talking about, it was dealing with people who were confident because they didn't know what they were talking about. The pups believed everything their parents taught them, and they did not know how to look at things any other way. Garth wanted to show them. He wanted to use this lesson to show them how to see more than one side and not dismiss anything contrary as nonsense.

That would require more time with the students, more discussion. Instead, Garth had to move them through the course material so they could be ready for the premade test at the end.

Some students chose books on war. Others chose books on general foreign policy. There were a lot of books about environmental issues. Most of the students had plagiarized book reviews from the internet. Garth didn't have to be a professional teacher to recognize writing that belonged to an adult book reviewer. What was the point in giving the assignment? He had no time to discuss this with anyone, and if they failed to do the analysis he wanted, what could he do? Fail them?

He worked the weekend on these papers, and now Garth understood why nobody did this. His workdays were full to the brim and he had no time to do anything that wasn't in the outline. His weekends were full enough recovering from the soul-sucking, mind-numbing week of repeating pre-designed lectures.

How could he make a better class? By the time the weekend rolled around, all he wanted to do was sleep. His paychecks were still coming up short of his student loan payments, and now he considered taking a night job.

Ten years in university, he thought, *Ten years and a PhD.*

After giving passing grades to everybody, Garth read the guide in more detail. He really was being forced to take part in his own obsolescence. Garth ignored the paper, crawled into bed and did not leave the apartment.

Foremost in his mind was the living hell it was going to be to do baseball next unit.

Chapter 16

The baseball unit had been going on for two weeks, and it was unfulfilling. Garth at least knew how to play the game, so he could engage the students a little more, but it was all so pointless. It did not prepare anyone for the real world. It did not encourage teamwork, as the outline claimed. Garth had always laughed at people who claimed sports encouraged teamwork and cooperation. Instead they only encouraged discrimination, telling students to perceive one another as winners and losers, those who could play well and those who could not.

He didn't have to do it every day though. Last week he had to fill in teaching two math courses instead of his usual gym units. Now he saw what Sasha was talking about. He didn't need to teach anything. The students knew all they had to do was plug in the answer choices into their calculators and that was it.

In the same way, Garth didn't need to know anything.

Garth went to work every day with this hanging over his head: he was disposable. He wasn't needed. At any time they could fire him and replace him with someone cheaper.

Garth procrastinated on the course outline. He thought he could remember a time, not too long ago, when he had wanted to go to work and do a good job.

He was worried that he did not have the desire to exercise anymore. He still did it because he knew he should, but his heart wasn't into it as much as before. Now that he barely saw the weight room in school anymore, he had to work out at the gym, and when he got home he didn't feel like going anywhere or doing anything. Being at school took so much out of him all he wanted to do was sleep as soon as he got home, and every minute of the weekend.

He worked on the outline in little snippets during his downtime in the science lab, or while the students did the lesson in class. He hoped there was still a chance someone would notice what he could do and promote him out of this place.

Today, Garth sat in his office after the last bell. It was Thursday, so he had lacrosse coaching and speech team duty. He didn't want to show his face to any of those students.

There was a knock at his office door. The door wasn't closed, so Garth turned around in his chair. Evan was standing in the door, leaning on the frame with one hand, a completely unlustful look on his face. His crotch was not obscene.

"You okay, coach?"

"I'm fine, Evan. Just got a lot of work to do."

"You don't seem like the same person as before. What happened?"

"It's called having a job, Evan. Gotta be places you don't want to be, doing things you'd rather not do, and have lots of time to think about all the things you could be doing if you didn't have to be there."

Evan pushed away from the door and walked away. Garth felt bad for turning him away like that, but it was for the best. He would learn eventually. He turned around and resumed training his replacement.

The baseball unit ended a week and a half later and once again, Garth gave tests. He tested everyone in gym and everyone in his Government Studies course, and everyone passed. Since part of the school's funding was also tied to test results, it was in the school's best interest to make the tests as easy as possible. The dumber the students were, the longer the school could stay open to keep pumping out unchallenged idiots. He pondered it for a minute, but his mind trailed off before the thought could stick.

The next units were badminton, tennis and volleyball. Garth had chosen to be one of the badminton coaches, and as the students in the gymnasium selected their units, Garth didn't even look at them. They weren't people to him anymore. They were things to be manipulated by class outlines.

Mrs. Sinclair left on maternity leave, and Garth was now in charge of speech team. He tried to get involved, tried to give critique and help the students along, but the students were better at giving critique and guidance than he was. All he did was provide the exercises, sit by the desk and make sure the students actually practiced. Garth envied their ability to perform.

With only an hour to debate, and with so many points to get through every day with scripts that effectively made the issues undebatable, the Student Council had completely degenerated into arguing over who had to fill the soda machines. Fewer and fewer students came to the meetings as the weeks passed. Evan stopped coming to the meetings. Quickly attendance fell to three people, then two, then one, Gina.

On that day, Garth had an idea. She and he could debate the issues on the list together. She was the most opinionated person in the group, and Garth really wanted to hear how she would do against an adult perspective.

But the school did not care if the students on the council thought the issues through. If the lacrosse team did not progress, they would yell at him for that.

Instead Garth told her there would be no meeting today. She was disappointed, but she had other things to do anyway. As Garth watched her walk out the door, he lamented what had happened. She really believed in what they were doing. She really thought it made a difference, and she wanted to be part of that. The school's Student Council program had done exactly what it was designed to do, which was to instill in the children a sense that democracy was ineffective, decisions were impossible to reach, and nothing they did made any difference. These students would take that attitude into the world with them.

Garth ran to the lacrosse field early and helped Terrance drill the students. They were getting better, but not nearly as fast as the outline said they should. He wondered who wrote this course, and if it had been edited later. Perhaps crippled.

Then, on a Friday, Garth was sitting in front of Ms. Lilith Dover's desk once again. He dreaded taking this seat, but he shut up and braced himself for whatever was to come.

"Hello again, coach," she said. "It's been forever since I saw you. I hope you're doing all right."

I hate this place I hate this place I hate this I hate this I hate this—

"Yeah, fine."

"Good, because I have another opportunity for you. Speaking of which, have you made any progress on the weight program outline?"

"I am close to finishing. It's pretty tedious, that's why it's taking so long."

"If it's good work, it's worth it. I have good news. I have a job for you in your field of study."

Garth's ears perked, "Really? What's that?"

"Given your qualifications, I think you can give us better class outlines for our science department than what the district provides."

"What?"

"I have spoken to some of the Board, and they agree. They want you to draft new class outlines for chemistry, physics, earth science and biology."

"Sounds interesting, what's it pay?"

"You're already being paid, Coach Hood."

"I'm paid for the classes I do and the pups I coach. I'm not paid to design courses, too."

"Coach Hood," she said, leaning forward in her chair. "As part of your employment contract, you agreed to be available for any task the faculty deems necessary. And this is necessary. It is part of your job."

"And you want me to do the entire science department?"

"You are qualified."

"Ms. Dover..." Garth began. He wanted to tell her to shove it, walk out the door and never come back, but his student loans tugged at his ballsack again and held his muzzle closed. "How long do I have?"

"Until the end of the school year, so no hurry at all. The Board will have to look over them and suggest changes, so it will take a lot longer anyway."

Changes... Garth thought.

"May I see the current outlines for the science courses?"

"I have them right here. Remember to use them as a starting point. The school wants to improve them. See the teachers for the books. Remember we contract to use a textbook, but the outlines never use the entire thing. Take a look at what the book has to offer and suggest material to include or exclude from the course."

She slid a small stack of papers to Garth, who took them and stood up. "I'll get started on this soon."

"Thank you, coach. Have a good weekend."

Garth walked out.

For the first twenty paces he was dead to the world, which was usual after a visit to the personnel director.

In the second twenty paces, the quiet voice in his mind began to speak up.

By the third set of twenty, the fur on his back began to rise.

By the time reached his office, he was growling.

It felt good to growl again.

He stepped into his office, tossed the stack on the desk and walked out. He became a robot for the next four periods and through lunch. He made Government Studies another study hall with assignment, and hid behind the monitor.

During the second period of Government Studies, Garth kept glancing at Evan in the back. The dobie was reading and writing. He was so happy, so devoted. He was given a task to do, he did it, and he was rewarded. To him, that's how the world worked.

Garth waited for the bell to ring. When the pups got up and filed out the door, Garth spoke up.

"Mister Silvers."

Evan looked at him and hesitated, pulled his backpack over his shoulders and walked up to the desk.

"Yeah, coach?"

"You staying after school today?"

"No, I don't have to be in practice today and I don't work out."

"Well, if you can, I'd like you to stay after. I have some concerns about your workout plan I'd like to address. Meet me in room five-twenty after school."

Evan looked puzzled at first, and then smiled. "Sure. I can be there."

"Good. I'll see you then. Have fun in badminton."

"You, too," Evan said as he joined the flood of students rushing to their next class.

Garth stood up. He looked down at himself and realized he hadn't changed into teacher clothes in several weeks. He was dressed like a coach even as he tried to teach Government Studies. Garth couldn't believe he let himself slip this far. He gritted his teeth, walked out of the classroom and joined the pups and kits moving through the hallways.

The last period of gym was rough because Garth had to watch the students try to play badminton. A few nets down was the volleyball unit, and Garth watched the coaches stand on the sidelines as the pups served the ball. The ball was in the air. The students on the other side of the net watched it arc down, watched it, watched it, and then the ball hit the floor.

"Point," shouted Paul.

The students threw the ball back to the other side, the team served, and the same thing happened again.

Garth shook his head. He had been ignoring it for a long time, and now he saw it again. He turned to his badminton students as they tried to do the same thing with a birdie. The serving team smacked it over the net, most everyone on the other side just stood there, afraid to move, afraid to do anything.

Garth knew what the solution was: one on one. Practice hitting the birdie individually at first, then work in team coordination. But these were gym students. They weren't here to learn teamwork, nor did they expect to have to put any effort into this. They were content standing around and passing the course. Garth couldn't give every student one on one, or even two on two, time because that would mean the other students had nothing to do in the meantime. Big as this gymnasium was, there still wasn't enough room for everyone to learn it the right way. Even if he tried to get the students more involved, there wasn't enough time to build them into proper teams.

So he did as the other coaches did until it was time to send everyone to the lockers. When the bell rang, Garth walked to his office and searched for his teacher clothes. After going through every drawer twice, he remembered he hadn't even brought teacher clothes. He wasn't sure when he stopped.

He felt naked walking through the halls, and he felt just as naked when he entered room five-twenty. A couple students were already here, working on the previous assignment, which the outline told him would likely take two hours to complete. He had a half hour of questions to fake his way through, and then he had to inspect the programs.

Garth sat down at the desk and observed. Someone raised his hand, and Garth walked to them, book in hand, and addressed their concerns. Ten minutes later there was a knock at the door. Garth faced the door and peered through the glass window. The smiling face of a dobie greeted him. Garth held up one finger, stood and reached for his whistle. He stopped just short of blowing it to get the class's attention, giggled at himself, let it fall back between his pecs.

"Everyone, just a moment."

The students looked at him as a group.

"I need to help another student for a little bit. Will all of you be okay without me?"

Some laughed. Some nodded. Some said, "Sure."

"No parties while I'm gone please. I will find out."

They laughed again, and resumed typing. Garth walked to the door, opened it, and slipped out.

"You wanted to see me."

"Yes, Evan, I saw you working out the other day and you're still squatting improperly. I want to show you how to do it right so you don't hurt yourself."

"Sure, Coach, thanks."

Garth walked him down the hall, around several corners and finally they reached the gym lockers. They were completely deserted, but Garth wasn't taking a chance. He led Evan to his office, pushed him inside and closed the door.

Evan turned around and smiled at him. He slipped his backpack off, which landed on Garth's desk. "I knew you couldn't keep away forever."

Garth growled, reached under the pup's arms, lifted him up and sat him down on the desk. Evan's paws were already on his shorts. Garth yanked them down, and now Garth saw his secret to keeping it obscene. He had a rubber band around one leg, and his cock was tethered down by it. He smiled.

"So that's how you do it."

Evan hadn't stopped smiling. "I can go from showoff to normal any time I want."

Garth hooked a claw under the rubber band and pulled it down, freeing Evan's dick form his leg. He kneeled on the floor and started rubbing it with both hands, squeezing it, feeling it as it stiffened and rose. Garth picked it up, opened his mouth and gulped it down, growling. It tasted so good. Evan meanwhile was rubbing his forearms. Garth flexed the muscles more than he had to as he suckled Evan until it was difficult to breathe. Garth withdrew and he looked at it, studied it in more detail. It wasn't all the way up yet.

"How the hell did I sit on this?" he said.

"You seemed determined," said Evan, leaning back on the desk, propping himself up against his backpack.

Garth reached down, lifted up his shirt and worked it over his head. He had a difficult time moving his arms like this, but he also knew what it looked like in the mirror, his muscles bunching up and getting in each other's way. Evan was captivated.

The mastiff tossed his shirt on the floor and stood before Evan, finally giving him the view he always wanted. Evan leaned forward, felt his stomach, his arms, his chest.

"Oh, I've missed this. Every time I'm in class all I wanted you to do was take off those clothes. They hide too much."

Garth reached down, pulled his shorts off. Evan looked down eagerly. Garth was already up and leaking. Evan lifted his legs and leaned back on the desk, cock resting on his chest. Garth growled, unzipped Evan's backpack, found the bottle and lubed his cock up. He held onto the pup's waist and pushed his cock in under Evan's balls. Evan moaned and leaned back, drinking in the view of the body that was entering him. The dobie was as ready as always, so Garth met with only moderate resistance before he was all the way inside.

Garth wasted no time. He pounded Evan's rear as fast as he wanted, gritting his teeth, not even thinking about anything else but taking what he had always wanted.

He looked down at Evan, penis resting on his ridiculously lithe body, touching his muzzle in this position. It excited Garth even more and he rammed Evan even deeper. The dobie laid still, the look on his face making all the sounds he wanted to make.

Garth leaned close to take in the pup's scent. Evan was about to lick his muzzle, but Garth leaned close to his ear.

"Show me how you suck yourself."

Evan let go of Garth's arms, grabbed his penis and moved it to the side. He leaned forward just slightly and took the tip in his own muzzle. It was even hotter than watching it grow from soft to monster. Garth pounded him faster, and it felt better than ever. The act folded Evan a little more and the dobie swallowed more of himself. The more he did, the harder Garth slammed him, trying not to growl too loudly.

Garth had never wanted to cum so badly in his life. He rammed Evan harder as he watched the young pup suck himself. He couldn't go deep enough, couldn't fuck him fast enough. He lay on the pup, feeling his dick against his chest and stomach, reminding Garth how much bigger it was compared to his own. It pushed him over the edge. He gritted his teeth, held his muzzle against the dobie's ear.

"Evan... I'm gonna cum. Take it all. You're fucking mine now."

Evan moaned, reached back and held Garth's rear, pulling him all the way inside. Garth thrust him once more and made up for lost time. Garth stayed all the way inside and laid on top of the pup as the mastiff filled him. Evan held Garth's arm with one hand and his own dick with the other, still sucking. He even moaned with a full mouth.

Garth rose up slightly, pulled Evan's cock out of his muzzle, opened wide and took as much as he could. Garth was going soft, but he stayed in Evan, trying to pound him more, wishing it wouldn't end. It must have done something for Evan, because after only a few thrusts, Evan erupted in Garth's muzzle. It was like Evan made up for lost time too, as this was the biggest load yet. Garth sucked it down and milked the entire length trying to get every last drop. When he was sure he had it all, he let go. It fell back to Evan's chest with a wet *thud*.

Garth withdrew. Evan still held him, and Garth laid his upper body over him, holding Evan by the waist, feeling him up. The mastiff smiled and growled. Evan now had his hands on Garth's chest. They lay like this for a while, taking in each other's scents.

"What made you change your mind?" said the dobie.

"I'll tell you later." He reached down, squeezed Evan as it softened. He grinned as he rubbed Evan up and down, squeezing even more cum out of him. Garth leaned down, slurped it up. "You had the guts to hit on a dog twice your age while still in school. That kind of ambition deserves a reward. Let's make this work."

"The stories I could tell you."

"I want to hear all of them, but right now I have to get back to class. Can't leave the students alone too long."

"Still afraid of someone noticing?"

"Nope. Fuck this place, but I still need the job."

Garth rose, bent over and picked up his shirt. Evan rose as well, lowering his legs, panting, taking in the view. The mastiff grinned, gave him another muscle show putting on his shirt.

"I love to see them moving," said the dobie.

"I'll move them for you all day whenever I can."

Smiling, Evan stood up, pulled up his rubber band and gym shorts.

Chapter 17

Garth stood on the field in front of the lacrosse players, holding the outline at their current place. They were in phase three: moving and passing. According to the outline, by this point, the players should be able to jog at a brisk pace while passing the ball between them.

The mastiff looked up from the paper. Two canines were jogging, one flung the ball out, and the other missed the catch. These were the two best players so far. The others were still barely able to walk and pass at the same time. Students were running up and down the field trying to pass and missing at every attempt. Garth turned to Terrance. The fat Mastiff just stood there, glaring at the players.

"The outline says we're supposed to start drilling them on team coordination."

"We'll start that tomorrow," Terrance said. "Give 'em one more day to get the hang of passing."

"They're not even close to ready."

"Not what the outline says."

"You know they're not ready."

"I ain't paid to think. I'm paid to give the course they hand me."

"You said they'd blame us if the students fail."

"As long as we follow the outline, they can't touch us."

"You sure about that?"

"That's one thing the union agreed to that I actually like. Say what you want about the union, but they knew this was coming and they tried to protect us from it. The school can't fire us for any damn reason thanks to them."

"But now we *have* to follow it, even when it doesn't work."

"Not our problem, Garth."

Garth shook his head. The weather was getting cold. Coming up soon they'd have to move practice indoors, and Garth did not look forward to that. It could only mean more injuries.

"How are the basketball teams?" Garth said.

"Doing all right. Most of 'em know what they're doing. I'd give anything to be with 'em more, make sure they're learning how to be a team. School wants us to make athletes out of these pups, and then they make us pull triple duty. It's like asking a farmer to build a barn and then taking away half his wood and blaming him for not making it work."

"This problem is easy to fix."

"Every problem is easy to fix. Just let us do our jobs. I keep tellin' 'em. Nobody listens. They get what they get. Watch 'em, Garth. I gotta piss."

Terrance turned and walked across the field to the school. Garth did not look back. He watched the students. They were trying. They really were. All they needed was more time and they'd get the hang of it. If they interrupted them now, they'd disrupt any progress these students had made.

Garth looked over his shoulder. Terrance was gone. Garth turned to the students, raised the whistle to his lips and blew. Everyone stopped, faced Garth. Garth raised his voice so the whole field could hear.

"Show of hands. Who here is comfortable with passing and running and is ready to move on to team coordination?"

The pups and kits looked around. Nobody raised their paws. Garth nodded.

"Gotta admit. We've been following the outline, and it says by now everyone here should be able to run and pass. Now I don't blame you for being behind schedule. I think the schedule is wrong. What do you say?"

They began nodding. The nodding spread, turned into a shout.

Garth smiled. "I agree. Let's go back to stationary passing. Everyone partner up, get in position, and Chris." A young fox looked at him. "Toss me that stick."

The fox picked up a spare stick from the grass and threw it to Garth. The mastiff caught it in one hand, threw his clipboard down and took a position with two students.

"I also gotta say. I have never played lacrosse before. I don't know why I'm here, but I say when I get to the point where I can catch and pass, then we all can start running."

The students laughed, shouted again. Garth shared a partner with Chris and they took turns catching and throwing the ball to the Labrador twenty feet away. Garth missed the ball his first three tosses, but so did Chris, and they laughed together. For the first time, he wasn't afraid to show the students he didn't know the game, and shouldn't be coaching it. Terrance never once said it would be a bad idea to reveal this, but it was heavily implied in the way Terrance almost never picked up a stick. The entire coaching experience had been merely watching the pups go through the different drills.

Now Garth was among them, practicing with them, an equal, not merely the observer spitting out prewritten advice. He started to get into it. After a dozen throws Garth started to get a feel for where the net was, and where his hands had to be to catch the ball. It still wasn't easy, and even after twenty throws Garth missed more than he caught, but all around him the students were glad to backtrack on the lesson and go back to doing this. It felt good to move. It felt good to be active and engaged in something again.

Garth switched partners and now he stood with a coyote, facing a pit-bull. Garth flung the ball to his partner. The ball fell short, rolled up to the pit-bull, who scooped it up and tossed it to the coyote. He caught it, served it back. The pit-bull missed, turned and ran after the ball.

"So coach," said the coyote, "you think we're gonna have a team at this rate?"

Garth laughed. "It's been a month. The guide we're following says you should be star players by now. I think the people who wrote the guide never played the game themselves." Garth blinked a few times, stood ready at the pit-bull lined up and raised his stick. "Oh, my name is Mister Hood."

The canine facing them threw the ball Garth's way. It was too high. Garth raised his stick and tried to catch it, but he underestimated.

The ball sailed over Garth's head, bounced six times and rolled in the grass. Garth turned and chased it. He picked it up, and as he rose he saw Terrance walking across the field. Garth smiled, turned around and ran back to his place in line, positioned himself and tossed the ball. It went long this time, and the pit-bull ran to retrieve it.

By now Terrance was behind Garth.

"Coach Hood?"

"They're not ready for the next lesson. I decided to go back to this. And my name is Mister Hood."

"A word with you... Mister Hood."

Garth nodded, turned around and walked with Terrance. When they were out of earshot, Terrance spoke softly.

"Maybe if the school had gotten some lacrosse players to coach these pups and give them some real instruction, they'd be ready by now, maybe, but so what. School gets what it pays for."

"Terrance, I want to fucking do a good job at something! I'm tired of standing around watching them. I want to get in there with them, help them, teach them right, do something besides stand here!"

"What do you care?"

"I should be in the weight room, not here, but we can fix this, Terrance. We can make this a decent team. All we need is to spend a little longer on the basics. Who's keeping track of where we are in the outline? Who's gonna know? All they care about is the results."

"I don't get paid enough to give them both a good basketball team and a good lacrosse team, and neither do you."

"God damn it, Terrance, I want to do something!"

"Do you want to prove the outlines work? If we turn those pups into a good team, they'll assume the course outlines work, and then they'll have an excuse to replace us."

"Forget the outline! Let's just coach them. We'll all learn this together. Then we can shove it in their faces when we do a good job without following the directions."

"Garth, I think you need a break."

"I don't need a break. I need someone to let me do a good job. I don't wanna be here, but I can do good work if someone lets me."

"Come back in twenty minutes, Garth," Terrance said, smacking him on the shoulder. "Get a drink or something."

He turned around and walked back to the students. Garth looked over his shoulder. Terrance was telling the students to start running and passing, and the players did not sound happy.

Garth closed his eyes, hung his head and walked back to the school. In five minutes he was inside the gymnasium. He stayed on the sidelines to avoid the volleyballs flying everywhere. The divider walls were up, separating the gymnasium into four separate courts, and Garth walked through the gaps between them. Volleyball was in the next partition. Soccer practice was in the next.

He walked into the locker rooms, rounded the corner and stepped into his office, pulling the door shut behind him. Evan was sitting at Garth's desk. His ears perked up when Garth came in.

"You're early!"

"Terrance told me to take a twenty minute break. I'll take half an hour."

Evan licked his lips, stood up and pulled Garth's shirt up. Garth raised his arms and allowed Evan to take it off for him, then tossed it in the corner with a flick of his wrist.

Garth stood before Evan. The dobie grinned and rested his palms on Garth's pecs, feeling all the way around them. Garth did not flex or pose. He just stood there, holding Evan at the waist. One paw migrated to his rear and squeezed.

"What'd you do to get a break?"

"Tried to do my job. Not even my job, but what I was told."

"They don't like it when you do your job?"

"They want it both ways. They'll tell you to do something and then get mad at you for doing it."

"Sounds dumb."

Garth rubbed Evan's arms up and down. As he did he growled, turned Evan around and bent him over the desk. Evan's tail wagged wildly as he pulled his shorts down. Garth opened a drawer in his desk, pulled Evan's bottle of lube out of it and prepared the dobie. Evan panted and moaned just from someone else touching him there, which Garth found absolutely adorable.

He dropped his own shorts, lubed himself up and pushed his cock in the dobie. Evan gasped and went to heaven. So did Garth. He pushed in until his hips met Evan's, and he stayed there for a moment. He didn't even want to fuck anything, just being here was enough.

"How long have you been doing stuff like this?" whispered the mastiff.

Evan moaned and panted just from Garth being here. "Since the seventh grade."

"That young? Wow. Who got you first?"

Evan giggled, propped himself up on his elbows and whispered to the wall. Garth rode him slowly.

"I... It was in gym glass. We were changing into shorts. This dog noticed I had a bulge and pointed it out to the others. They laughed at it. Ganged up on me, pulled my undies off."

Garth had thrust into him three times while he spoke so he wouldn't be so distracted. "What did they think when they saw that sausage between your legs?"

"They stopped laughing. They just stared. Finally I pulled 'em back up and changed shorts."

"Weren't you embarrassed?"

"You know... I wasn't. I don't know why. Maybe it was me seeing their shocked stares. They stopped picking on me."

"What happened then?"

Evan giggled as Garth pushed all the way. The giggle blended into another trip to heaven. "One of the dogs came to see me later. He offered to show me his if I'd show him mine again."

"Where?"

"He found me after school. I went to his place, showed it to him. He showed me his. We were both hard as flagpoles, but I had him beat by twice as much."

Garth smiled, thrusting into Evan a little faster, reaching down and stroking the dobie's pole. The dobie reached down and held Garth's hand as he did.

"I don't even remember how he ended up inside of me. Don't even know how we figured out we could do that and that it might feel good. It just happened. He was one of the dogs that shoved me around all the time. We were friends for a while after that, until he moved."

"Evan, you are so lucky, and not just for this." He squeezed his dick a few times, thrust into him shallow, then deep. "You happened to meet another pup who was interested and not afraid to explore. You don't even know how rare that is."

"I didn't even know what that meant until later! We were totally innocent, just doing whatever felt good. It was all so new and everything felt good."

Garth picked up the pace. Evan took it like a champ, smiling so big Garth could see it from behind.

After a while, they heard voices and the slamming of locker doors. Evan looked back at Garth and grinned. The mastiff grinned back, and thrust into Evan slower. Evan closed his mouth and moaned with his whole body instead of his voice. Garth moaned and growled with his hips.

As the locker room chatter and metal-on-metal sound became louder, Garth rammed Evan faster. Evan held Garth's hand as Garth felt the dobie's pole up and down. Suddenly Terrance's voice broke up the chatter and the lockers were silent.

"All right, everyone, I just told the girls this, now it's your turn. Thursday we start getting coordinated as a team. Don't worry about not being able to throw or catch the ball. You'll learn as we go."

Garth tried not to laugh, and fucked Evan harder. The dobie muffled his moans on Garth's bicep, licking the veins under the short fur. Terrance went on about the importance of coordination and trust. Garth recognized it. He had read that part of the outline that told him to say those exact words at this exact time. The course outline did not, however, specify where to deliver this speech, and the mastiff was surprised Terrace had thought of doing it in the lockers on his own. Perhaps he checked with the higher-ups first.

Just as Terrance finished his speech, Garth finished in Evan. He stayed deep as he did, making sure he seeded the pup good. Evan licked Garth's arm all around. Garth waited until the locker room began swelling with noise again and pulled out. Evan rose from the desk and turned around. Garth went down to his knees, and Evan held the back of the mastiff's head and pushed his cock into Garth's muzzle. The mastiff rubbed it up and down and sucked it. Evan finished in five seconds, and he held Garth's muzzle down. Garth had to swallow, even if he choked on it. As Garth sucked it down, Evan felt his arms from shoulders down to the wrists.

Evan released Garth, and he stood up. They both stood there, grinning at one another as the players gradually left the lockers. Evan felt Garth up, Garth felt Evan up, both getting hard again. Evan leaned against the desk, crossing swords with the bigger dog.

When there was no more noise, Garth spoke quietly. "We're not allowed to think for ourselves here. All they want us to do is whatever the outline says. I'm not allowed to go the extra mile around here. Don't believe what they tell ya, Evan. Being a good employee is not rewarded these days. They'll just fire the lazy dog and dump his work on you."

Evan didn't seem to hear him. He reached around, embraced Garth, burying his muzzle between Garth's pecs. Garth held him, felt his rear and fingered his hole. Evan clung to him tighter.

Chapter 18

Garth pulled his paw out of the slot in the wall that was his mailbox. In it was the usual list of Student Council issues, followed immediately by his scripts.

1. If the school should consider offering an alternative lunch for felines. / *A governing body should encourage others to provide for themselves.*

2. If the school should consider installing a Golden Halo restaurant in its cafeteria instead of the cafeteria staff / *Students should consider revenue benefits to the school, labor savings, and current food quality and whether the proposal would be better for the students.*

3. Whether teachers should be required to offer alternative assignments to athletes to compensate for their busy schedules. / *The council is reminded to debate carefully the performance of the athletes.*

4. Soda machine duty.

5. There has been a proposal to add a new machine to the cafeteria that would vend school supplies. / *Projected revenue from this new machine is expected to pay for the machine's installation and energy costs in less than a semester.*

Garth shook his head. It was nothing but loaded debate. He was there to steer to the students to agree with whatever the higher-ups had already decided. Not only that, they were starting to repeat issues.

He wasn't sure what to expect this Wednesday. Would there be a student council anymore? What was Garth supposed to do about it? Without that hour of his time, he could actually be in the weight room, supervising the A-shift. The idea that he might actually be able to do his job excited him, and hurt him at the same time.

Garth had read two chapters ahead in the Government Studies book over the weekend, so he at least seemed like he wasn't reading from the book completely. Last night, he came across an article on the net, and he saw a chance to change up the class.

During his first Government Studies course, the students took out their books, preparing for Garth's usual read-along. This time, however, Garth handed a stack of papers to the first student in each column of desks.

"Pass it back. Honestly, everyone, I'm bored. This is getting way too routine. School wants me to follow the book to the letter, but today we're going to read something different. I found this article online and I thought I would share it with all of you."

Garth leaned on the desk, paper in hand, and read.

The article was about the enormous amount of money campaigns for government office cost these days. The article proposed that this kept the average person from running for public office, as in modern times, only the rich (or a person who had rich connections) could afford to even consider running. The article went on to say it was time to reform the system, to make all campaigns for public office publically funded, and at a flat rate with no outside contributions.

The students still had that look on their faces that betrayed their secret desire to be texting instead.

"So what do you think?" Garth said, probably the most un-teacher like thing he could have said to start things off. "Anyone hear much about campaign costs these days?"

Nobody spoke.

"Well I'll tell you what I know. It was ridiculous even when I was in high school, and it's only gotten worse. So why do you think so much money goes into campaigns these days?"

All was silent for a moment, and then one canine in the middle row spoke. "Television?"

"What do you mean television?"

"Well... like..."

He stammered for a bit. Garth contemplated that this must be the noise the brain makes when it's working hard, like a car starting on a cold morning. This dog's brain probably hadn't been started since grade school.

"It's... you know... there's so much... you know..."

Garth smiled. "Don't say you know. Just speak."

"There's just... There's so much out there. You got... You got like the internet, radio..."

"Right!" Garth said. "There's more media than ever these days. It costs money to get on everything. That's one reason campaign spending is bigger than ever. It's going to as more media becomes available. There are other reasons though."

Garth had no idea what those other reasons were off the top of his head. He was hoping one of the students would come up with something.

One of the ladies raised her hand. Garth called on her. She lowered her paw, and sat cross-legged with both paws in her lap again.

"It's kind of a competition thing. One guy spends a million, so the other has to, and then the other has to spend two million."

"Yes!" Garth said. "Very good! It is a competition for the office, so there will be competitive spending. Combine that with more media and it's just a mess. What do you think? Does this impact who can run?"

Someone else spoke up. Garth looked around the room and noticed the bored appearances were all but gone. Some of the students were waking up, as if for the first time since the school year began.

Garth was surprised. Some of them had actual thoughts on the subject. He never would have guessed, with the way they lazed around in class, but many of them did have opinions, and Garth addressed them individually, never outright refuting them, but trying to present another point of view.

Garth still didn't know what he was talking about, but he was older and had seen more of this than the students, so he debated them on a more personal level. He hoped he wasn't coming across as a teacher who knew more than everyone, but merely an adult.

Garth wasn't sure what the merits of publically funded elections would be, but he was glad to listen to their opinions. He assigned today's chapter as homework and promised a quiz on the chapter tomorrow. He also told the students to search for opinions on the merits and drawbacks to publically funded elections, and what it would mean for the political process.

As the next Government Studies class entered, Garth was eager and confident now. He stood at the desk, waiting for everyone to take their seats. Evan was being modest today, and Garth was glad for that.

He passed out the papers, read the article, and got the students talking about an actual issue relevant to today's world. For the second time in a row, the class woke up from its collective stupor. The students expressed opinions. Those opinions led to more ideas. The ideas led to other ideas, and they debated the idea of publically funded elections. Garth assigned today's chapter, and also told them to do research on the idea.

As the bell rang and Garth gathered his things, he happened to notice the student council issue list on the desk. He looked up. Evan was just getting ready to walk out the door.

"Mister Silvers."

Evan stopped. The students behind him filtered around him and into the hall.

"Do you know any of the student council members?"

"Yeah, I know a few of 'em."

"Do me a favor will you? Tell them there will be a meeting on Wednesday. I promise what happened to it over the last few weeks will not happen again. Make sure they show up, please. I have some real issues for them to talk about. They're important."

Evan smiled. "I'll tell them."

Garth smiled, nodded to the door, and Evan joined the students in the hall. The mastiff rose from the chair and walked to his office to change clothes.

After school, in the programming course, Garth was trying to make the program he had assigned the students, without looking at what the code should be. He had read enough of this stuff over the last few weeks, and he thought he knew what to do by now. It wasn't easy, as he had to work between questions the students had. Debugging code without knowing the code was a challenge, but all the mistakes he saw were simple enough to identify.

When that hour was up, the abbreviated speech team session met. The students were already here, already about to start where they left off yesterday. Garth looked around, and wondered about the obvious question he had not thought to ask in a long time.

"Everyone, are you okay with me going somewhere else for a few minutes?"

They nodded, shrugged their shoulders.

"Great. I'll be back shortly."

Garth closed the door behind him and walked around the school to the gym. He turned the corner, entered the gymnasium and walked down the sidelines straight for the weight room. There were only two students in here, one spotting the other on bench press.

"Where is everyone?" Garth said.

The dog spotting the other looked up at Garth and smiled.

"Coach Hood! Where've you been?"

"Nice to see you again!" said the dog on the bench.

"A-shift workouts are supposed to be here!" Garth said. "Where are the others?"

"Coach Bob's been keeping us for extra practice," said the student on the bench. "He let us come here 'cause we're the biggest."

"What?" Garth noticed it was true. They were the biggest two on the wrestling team.

"Yeah, he wants us to keep working out and he's training up the other students to be more agile."

"How long has this been going on?"

"A few weeks now."

Garth stood holding the door, unsure how he was supposed to feel. "Thanks." He pushed away and ran along the sidelines, through the dividers and found the overweight fox watching two of the students wrestle on blue mats.

"Bob!" Garth shouted.

Everyone halted, stared at the large mastiff walking up to the fox. He passed the mats and stood snout to snout with the coach.

"What the hell are you doing?! They're supposed to be lifting weights!"

"We got competition season starting, Garth. Now's the time to practice, not work out."

"You only got two of your students in there! Where's the football team? Where's the rest of the wrestling team?"

"Competition season is starting for football, too. Gotta work on being a team, not bulking up."

"My job's on the line here! Get those pups back in the weight room!"

"We already talked about this," Bob said. "Workouts are taking too much time away from practice. First they need to be a team. Then they can bulk up."

"Do you want them ready for competition? Keep them in the weight room now!"

"Got my two main dogs in there. They'll be ready."

"The school wants everyone to put on some mass before competition starts, not just the dogs who already have it!"

"Do you want to take this to my office?"

"There's nothing to discuss! Get those pups back on weights!"

"Look, Garth, if we lose any more competitions, my job's on the line. I don't want to lose any more days because the school thinks my pups need to start exercising. It's stupid, Garth, and you know it."

"It's my job."

"So why are you on speech team and computer lab?"

"I'd rather be in the weight room with those pups."

"I'd rather be somewhere else, too. Take it up with Ms. Dover, and good luck."

Garth turned away and left the gym, clenching his fists as he stormed down the hall. He stopped by the offices, but to his surprise, Ms. Dover was not in the office. Garth's mind took a solid minute to accept this. He had never imagined Ms. Dover anywhere else but her office.

Garth stormed out, and by the time he reached Mrs. Sinclair's classroom he had calmed down enough to show his face to the students. He took a seat behind the desk and watched the students rehearse their speeches.

Forty-five minutes later, the busses arrived, and Garth watched the students leave. He remained at the desk for a little while longer, rubbing his forehead. A moment later, he smelled dobie in the room.

Garth faced the door. Evan was leaning on it with one hand, holding his backpack strap with the other.

"What did you say to Coach Bob?" Evan said. "He was mad after you left."

Garth stood up, walked to the windows and drew the blinds one by one. "Why didn't you tell me nobody had been doing the workouts?"

"I thought you knew. I mean, they took you out, so I thought they'd been cancelled."

"No, Evan. They weren't cancelled. I'm still responsible."

"Sorry."

"Eh, not your fault. Just fuck me."

Evan smiled, pulled the door closed behind him and removed his backpack. Garth removed his shorts and began pulling his shirt up, facing the desk. Evan walked up to him from behind, helped him lift the shirt off all the way, and felt Garth's back.

"Do you always keep your fur this short?" said the pup, running his fingers through the separation of the muscles all over his back.

"Usually, yeah."

Evan's paws migrated around to Garth's chest, squeezed his pecs, trying to grip the whole muscle. He pushed Garth forward. Garth bent over the desk, tucking his arms in, trapping Evan's hands on his chest.

"Your tits are so big I can't get my hands on them!"

"I don't have tits." Garth said, tail waving. "Hurry up and get in me."

"I need one hand."

"All right, one." Garth lifted his left arm just enough for Evan to slip out.

Garth felt the tip slide under his tail and gritted his teeth. Evan spread him wide open as the doberman slid into the mastiff. Garth tried not to make any noise. Evan knew how big he was, and he knew the damage he could do. He did not shove it all the way in, but pumped it in gradually, back and forth, going in a little deeper each time. Garth felt every in-thrust in his gut. Clenching his muzzle shut didn't help. He muffled his moaning on his own bicep.

Evan slipped his hand under Garth's arm. Garth clamped it again and Evan's paws were trapped on Garth's pecs. He flexed and puckered them for him. Evan held on and thrust deeper and deeper. Garth did not think his bicep made a good muffler.

The thrusting now tingled his gut, and it did not feel like a good thing. He lifted his muzzle from his arm.

"That's deep enough. Holy shit far are you?"

"A little more than halfway."

"That's it!?"

"You want me to stop?"

"Yeah. Just fuck me like this."

"But our balls aren't touching. We're not gay yet."

"You're using my pecs as leverage. Close enough. Damn, Evan, you're a challenge. Pisses me off I can't take it all."

"It's only your third try."

Garth was about to respond but Evan gripped Garth's chest and pulled out, then squeezed his pecs and used his chest to push himself in again. Garth shifted his arms, made his muscles move for Evan, made his chest and arms bulk up even more. It drove Evan wild, and he fucked Garth as hard as Evan wanted to be fucked, being careful not to go too deep. He did several times, and Garth had to accept the spearing, nauseating feeling in his gut.

Evan lasted a very long time, but so did Garth.

Chapter 19

Garth turned the corner and stared. There was a line coming out of the door to the offices. He approached the last dog in line and tapped her on the shoulder.

"What's this?"

"The Dover lineup."

"Everyone's here to see Ms. Dover?"

"Yup."

"Does she run the school?"

"She may as well."

"Shit."

"I know."

"I think I'll come back."

"Smart."

Garth turned around and walked the way he came. He didn't feel disappointed at all. He never expected taking the issue up with her to change anything, but he decided to try later.

His time in the badminton unit was boring and uninteresting, and for the first time he realized he looked forward to Government Studies.

After four periods of watching pups and kits trying to smack a birdie over a net, and getting maybe one or two volleys out of each serve, Garth was ready for something that required thought. He changed into his teacher clothes, ate lunch, and sat in the classroom and waited.

He gave the usual quiz for the book material they were supposed to read yesterday, and then jumped right into what he had wanted to do all day. To his surprise, some of the students actually did the assignment, and came back with their own thoughts on the subject. Garth had ideas of his own, and he ran them by the class.

How should the amount of funding be determined? How should it be spent? Should there be allocated amounts to each media source? Could a specific website be created, or a specific time slot on TV devoted to political campaign ads? Would this violate free speech? Should candidates be allowed to receive additional funds from any other source, and how would this be enforced? Would this truly level the playing field and keep money out of politics?

It wasn't teaching so much as thinking aloud to other people. Some of the students responded to the ideas and came back with thoughts of their own. Most of the students didn't want to do anything but think about texting, but Garth did not look at them. He focused on six who responded to stimulus, and talking about something happening right now did the trick.

His second period of Government Studies went even better, with Evan contributing many thoughts and attitudes. Garth was thrilled to be engaged with them. He didn't feel like a person behind a desk giving them material, but a partner going through a process with them. By the time class was over, Garth wanted to feel this way forever.

After his last gym period, Garth changed clothes, ran back to the classroom and waited for the student council to show up. Four students came, half the usual crowd, Evan and Gina among them. Garth could be happy with that.

"Thanks for coming back," Garth said to the small group. "I'm sorry about what happened over these last few weeks. I promise I won't let it happen again, and to prove it, here's the first point I want to address. You've already debated it. Should the school offer an alternative lunch for the felines? Anyone remember what we agreed to?"

"Yeah," Gina said. "You said the school can't afford it, so it's up to the cats to find their own food."

"That's what I said, yes, but that's not all of it. Let me give you something new to work with. What if forcing people not in the majority to fend for themselves isn't the same as taking responsibility? Ask yourself why these budget cuts are happening in the first place, and are they using some moral ideal as a means to divert attention from why the school has such a limited budget in the first place?"

The students did not follow that at all.

"Think about it," Garth continued. "They cut the budget to the school lunches, and now they turn around and tell the felines it's their responsibility to provide for themselves. School had no problem providing for them before the budget cuts, but now all of a sudden it's a moral issue. It's not. It's money. Now, with that said, it's not going to change by a simple vote. The school really does have a limited budget and it's too late to fix that. If anyone really wants it to change, something bigger has to happen. Which brings me to the second point on the list, the school is apparently considering placing a Golden Halo in the cafeteria."

This got their attention. Ears perked up, and faces brightened.

"I'm supposed to tell you to consider revenue benefits for the school, labor savings and current food quality and whether the proposal would be better for the students. What do you think?"

"Well that's great!" Gina said. "Maybe we'd finally get some good food."

The students began to talk about the issue. It was good to see them debating, and Garth didn't feel guilty for shutting them down with a script. This time, he had used to script to stimulate debate, and now he would add his own script to the issue. They debated for a good ten minutes.

"Seems everyone agrees this would be a good thing," Garth said when they seemed to have exhausted themselves. "You all agree the food is bad, therefore we should just replace the cafeteria with a fast food place. But again, they're using the quality of the food to justify this change. Why is the food bad to begin with? Because they cut the budget. They created the problem, and now they're offering a solution. A solution that happens to involve firing the kitchen staff and outsourcing the cafeteria to lower-paid employees the school doesn't even have to pay."

"But the food will have to be better," Gina said.

"I don't believe that. It's fast food. And what do you think will happen to the prices? They're going to go up. Maybe not at first, but the restaurant will have no competition. They can charge the students anything they want, and since the school gets a kickback, it will be in their best interest to do so. For the lower-income students, this will hurt a lot. Pretty soon they'll be expected to just take responsibility for themselves and bring their own food."

"Well, that's the way it works now," Gina said. "Don't like the food, bring your own."

"That's true," said Garth, "and that's always an option. But think about this. Do you want the cafeteria to be a business, or a public service? Is education a business, or a public service? That's the only reason this is even being considered. Someone is setting themselves up to make money off of it. Don't think of it as a moral choice, or how it will benefit the students. Think about how it will benefit whoever owns this Golden Halo, and what they will do once they're here."

After forty-five minutes of debate, Garth moved on to the next point, whether teachers should be required to offer alternative assignments to athletes. His script wanted him to remind the students how important the athletic program is to the school.

"But again, any time someone tells you to think of one group of people, think about how it affects something else. Ever watch the news, how they like to talk about how something affects the children? They do that to get under your emotions so you stop thinking. What alternative assignments is it talking about? Crossword puzzles in math class instead of real assignments? Funny how they want the felines to take responsibility for themselves, but the athletes get special assignments that won't take time away from the game. The felines cost money, the athletes generate money."

"It's stupid," said Evan. "Won't do them any favors if they don't learn anything but how to catch a ball."

"Well it can be a lot of work," Gina said. "Keeping up with schoolwork and practice and all that pressure."

They had a real debate, and it lasted half an hour. Garth was supposed to be with Terrance for lacrosse, but he did not interrupt. Opinions ranged from no special consideration at all, to grading the athletes separately on a curve. Garth listened to them debate for a while. This lasted all but the last five minutes of their remaining time.

Garth picked up the paper and moved down to the next point. "We won't have time for the last point, but there's one more thing I want to say, about the soda machines."

The students rolled their eyes and moaned.

"Wait, wait, I want to give you something to take home. An idea. Volunteering your time is great, but at what point does it become extortion? You know people get paid to fill the machines, and yet the school wants you pups to do it for free, for the good of the school. Why? Who's benefiting? Who's saving money by making you work for free? Don't be fooled. If you want to volunteer, make sure it's for a good cause you believe in, and not because someone just wants free labor. Do not give your work away. You are all worth more than that."

It was time to go. The students packed their bags and stood up.

"We ran short, so we'll vote on these issues next meeting. Tell the other members we're meeting again and bring them back next week please."

They filed out the door. Garth's throat was dry and he was out of breath. Exhausted, but in a good way. He left the classroom, walked a little ways down the hall and stopped at the water fountain.

He heard claws clicking towards him. Garth turned his head and drank from an angle. Terrance was walking down the hall. Garth pretended to need more water.

"Coach Hood!"

Garth swallowed and rose upright. "Mister Hood."

Terrance stood way closer than interview distance. "You skipped lacrosse practice."

"Sorry, the student council was having a good debate and I didn't want to interrupt them."

"I needed you, Garth."

"No, you don't. The pups needed me here."

"Student Council is a joke. Don't skip out on me like that again."

"Lacrosse is a joke. This whole damn school is a joke. I had the chance to give those pups a real meeting, and I took it. I'll probably do it again next week. You can handle lacrosse by yourself, since you don't listen to me anyway."

"I'm just doin' my job."

"So am I."

Terrance stood there for a moment. Garth waited for him to say something. When he didn't, Garth walked past him and into the Government Studies classroom. He expected the overweight mastiff to follow him, but instead he heard claws clicking on the floor down the hall. Garth sat down at the desk and smiled.

The door closed. Evan had been hiding behind it, and he stood against the wall and smiled, too.

"You're making everybody mad this week."

"And it feels so good." Garth began undoing his pants as he walked to the chair behind the desk. Evan smiled, dropped his backpack and walked to the desk. He removed his pants and rubber band, unzipped his bag, removed the lube and slicked himself up. Garth was already naked from the waist down. He sat in the chair and faced Evan. The smaller dog climbed onto his lap and sat down on his cock, bracing himself on Garth's chest.

Garth let the dobie do all the moving, and Evan rode Garth slowly and quietly, savoring it, enjoying feeling Garth through his shirt.

"What do you plan to do after high school?" said the mastiff.

"College. Was thinking... either business or finance."

Garth laughed. "Is that what you want to do?"

"Well, no, but you can make good money."

"Once everyone has a degree in it, nobody will be able to make any money at it. Think about it a little more."

Evan rode Garth slowly, passionately, not like the times before, when it was sex they both needed, and moved in for the attack. Now it was sex they savored, and they wanted it to last. The more times he did this with Evan, the more it felt like intimacy instead of release. Garth held Evan's waist as the dobie rode him. His dick poked Garth in the muzzle, and he opened up and let it in.

Garth checked the door multiple times as Evan speared himself. After the third time, he realized he was hoping someone would walk in. He wanted everyone to see what he was doing. He wanted everyone to know he was fucking a student and loving it.

Evan finished quickly, despite how slow he'd been going. Garth was used to his volume and sucked it down fairly easily. He let Evan's dick go and looked the dobie in the eye. Evan's eyes were dreamy and delirious, but happy.

Garth reached under Evan's arms, picked him up just enough to lift him off his lap but not enough to slip off Garth's dick, and laid him on his back across the desk. He held Evan down by the shoulders, and now he controlled the spearing. Evan's eyes were buried in Garth's chest and arms as Garth plowed him as fast as Evan had fucked him the other day.

Evan's eyes had not moved from Garth's pecs the whole time, so Garth brought them closer. He lay his whole upper body on Evan and thrust him as deep as he could go. Evan's face really was buried in Garth's chest now, and Evan had nowhere to go while Garth rammed him.

He reached behind Evan, held him to his chest and rode him slower now. Evan was used to a pounding, but now Garth didn't want to. He wanted the pup to enjoy it. He thrusted into him slowly, tenderly. Evan gasped and held Garth, wanting Garth to be closer to him.

Garth checked the door one more time. Nobody had come in, and nobody could see them from this angle. The better it felt, the faster Garth wanted to pound Evan. As he picked up the pace, Evan moaned deeper, embracing Garth harder. He wasn't feeling his muscles anymore. Hadn't been for most of this time. He wasn't getting off to just a muscle dog anymore. He was getting off to Garth himself now. Realizing this made Garth want to thrust harder and harder. Evan held him tighter, moaning as loudly as he dared.

"Oh Garth, fill me up. Please."

Garth growled.

"Yeah, that's it, own me. Make me yours again."

Garth growled louder, thrust faster and faster. He opened his mouth and snarled as his hips tingled and his cock released. Garth stayed deep inside Evan when he climaxed. Evan held him tighter as Garth filled him up, whimpering and licking Garth's muzzle. Garth's arms were around the dobie. They lay like this for several minutes, Garth checking the door every few seconds. He wished someone had walked in so they could know how amazing this was.

Chapter 20

Garth sat opposite Ms. Dover. It had come to the point where Garth hated Fridays as much as he hated Mondays. It seemed too perfect to be coincidence—this had to be a management trend designed to punish employees for not devoting seven days a week to their jobs.

"I wanted to status with you on the course outlines," Ms. Dover said. "How are they progressing?"

Garth's ear twitched. Stepping into this office was like stepping into another country, with its own language and customs, most of them unwritten and secret, and with stiff penalties for breaching them.

"Progress is slow. Weekends are the only time I have a chance to work on them."

"I see. Well, please don't forget about them."

"You said there was no hurry."

"I just want to remind you of their importance."

"Sure."

"And I also have this for you." She slid a paper Garth's way. "It will replace your periods one through four gym class."

English I

Garth blinked, stared at the poodle. "You want me to start teaching an English course?"

"Until further notice."

"What happened to the teacher who was teaching it?"

"We have to move her to another area. Don't worry, it's all in the outline attached, even marked with where the last teacher left off. All you have to do is follow it."

Garth was about to say something, but Ms. Dover kept talking.

"Which reminds me, I wanted to touch base with you on a couple issues that have been brought to my attention. First, I have heard that the soda machines have been empty. Have you been following your scripts for the Student Council, Coach Hood?"

"Mister Hood, please. And yes, I have, but the last couple sessions we didn't quite get to that point."

"I see. Please make that your priority going forward. If the students can't fill it, that job falls to you."

"Now you want me to fill the soda machines? When am I supposed do that?"

"I am sure you will make the time. I also want to remind you to follow your outlines for Government Studies. I have heard chatter that implies you have not been."

"I have given the book as homework and reserved class time for discussion on some articles I found online. The classes have really gotten into it. They're talking, they're active, and they're interested in the material now."

"The course outline specifies you are supposed to teach the lesson, Mister Hood. Deviating from it is discouraged."

"The course outline wants me to read the exact same lesson in class I gave them for homework the other day. They are bored! I could give them an awesome class! There are students in that class who want to be engaged! They want to think! I'm giving them something to think about. All the school has to do is let me."

"Please stick to the course outline, Mister Hood. It is what you were hired for. And speaking of that, the results from the nurse are in, and the gains are less than expected."

Garth laughed. "Of course they are! The wrestling and football coaches stopped the workouts."

"I see. What have you done to correct this?"

"Me? Lilith, I'm not in the room anymore! You—or, the school took me out of the room weeks ago, and now the other coaches are taking the pups away from the weights so they can practice more. I could be doing my job and keeping those pups on the program, but I gotta do other people's work instead. I was going to ask you about that. Can you get the other coaches to put the pups back on the weights?"

"Mister Hood, your responsibility is to keep the students on the program."

"I want to do it! I want to do a good job! Take some of this other crap off of me so I can!"

"As I said before, those tasks will not change."

"How can they expect me to do the job when I'm not allowed to be in the room?"

"The school encourages a little competition between different departments. We feel each department will be freer to act in its best interest, and push every department higher, if it has the freedom to do so."

"What?! Now we're competing with each other?"

"It is a strategy that has succeeded in many other fields."

"This is a school! What good will competing do?"

"Mister Hood, I have faith in you. I know you can get this done."

Garth rose out of his chair, picking up the small packet of papers and stormed to his office. There were still ten minutes until school began, and he had only that long to put on the appearance that nothing was wrong. He looked forward to meeting Evan after school. It was the only thing that had kept him from sleepwalking through the last week.

There was little he could do during badminton to engage the students. There were too many of them and not enough equipment. He had plenty of time to wonder where the previous English teacher went, and now he was certain he had gotten into this just before teachers were replaced with interns who could move freely between classes as needed, each following scripts and none knowing what they were doing.

In time they would replace the interns with moderators, give the students the books and tell them to read. Then online videos would replace all the teaching. No thought. No challenge. Just watch and memorize and then get a job. Of course they'd be encouraged to go to college to improve their situation, but it would only be more of the same. Garth imagined a time in the future when public school had a stigma, and those who graduated from it would be trapped in the ditches while everyone who could afford better became the managers and technology workers.

And Garth was part of it.

He continued the debate from where he left off yesterday in both Government Studies classes. The discussion had moved on from campaign reform to foreign policy, something Gath knew absolutely nothing about, but the six students who actually wanted to do more than sleepwalk through the day wanted to talk about it, so Garth assigned everyone to find something to bring to the discussion on Monday. He hoped Lilith Dover would hear about this assignment and bring him to the office next week for another chat.

Garth was too busy trying to teach programming to search articles on the subject.

When the second set of late busses arrived, Garth walked back to his office in the locker rooms. Evan was sitting in his chair, holding the course outline for English I.

"They want you to teach an English course?"

Garth closed the door and locked it. "It'll be easy. All I have to do is follow the outline." He removed his shirt, started removing his pants.

"So is Mrs. Kri leaving?"

"I don't know what's happening to her. I'll ask her if I can. Or you can."

Garth had removed his pants. He was hard already just hearing Evan's voice. Evan pretended not to notice.

"So you're not gonna be in the gym at all?"

Garth was naked, and he grabbed Evan's shirt and started to undress him as well. Evan sat passively in the chair, lifting his arms to help, still reading the paper.

"Looks like it. I'll only do gym for one period a day. That's kind of a good thing, but now I have to fake teaching an English course."

"Why you?"

"I don't know. Sometimes I think they do it this way on purpose. Keep me so busy I don't have time to think about it."

He threw Evan's shirt in the corner, grabbed the dobie under the arms and stood him up. Evan still held the paper up.

"Well at least all the assignments are automatically graded."

Garth laughed. "They turned what should have been a timesaving invention into an excuse to dump more work on me."

Evan now stood naked, halfway hard himself. Garth turned him around, bent him over the desk, reached into one of the drawers and lubed both of them up. Evan was still holding the paper as Garth held his torso down.

"This doesn't make sense. They took you away from the weights and now you have to do this, too?"

Garth wrapped his arms around Evan, aimed himself and slipped in. Evan moaned, let the paper drop to the desk. Garth pushed all the way in, and lay on top of Evan.

"I'm not worried about it," Garth said. "It's Friday. I'm gonna have a good weekend coming up with more ways to make people mad."

He pulled out, pushed in. Evan held onto the far edge of the desk and moaned. Garth rubbed Evan's cock up and down, hoping Evan would shoot all over the office.

Chapter 21

The *English I* class was at the beginning of some classic novel Garth had neither heard of nor encountered in all his years in university. The outline called for Garth to go through analysis of the previous day's chapter. He had not been given the novel ahead of time to catch up to where the class was in the book, so Garth had no idea what the points were, but he gave a lecture and read the points.

Garth read the excerpts and explained these were examples of certain themes. Other excerpts demonstrated stylistic choices in the writing, such as apostrophe and authorial interjection. Another point expanded on the symbolism. Garth read the lesson, not understanding a word of it, but the students did not seem to notice. Most of the students had read it, so they answered the questions as if Garth would understand the answers.

Garth finished the lesson, assigned the students to read the next chapter and sat behind his desk. He wanted to read the book himself, but he didn't want to be seen reading it now. Admitting he didn't know what they were reading seemed like a bad idea.

He had asked around before school, and found out that Mrs. Kri had been moved to social studies because another teacher, Mrs. Zug, was out on medical leave. Sasha Grace had been pulled out of her math classes to fill in for the other English courses that Garth could not teach because he was in Government Studies.

Garth was put off that Ms. Dover had not simply mentioned this. All she had to do was say Mrs. Zug was out on medical leave and they needed him to fill in, but no, she had given a cryptic answer and Garth had to find out the real reason by rumor. Something about the underhandedness of it did not sit well with the mastiff.

As Garth watched the students read he contemplated that the school was so cheap they didn't even want to pay for a substitute teacher, so they simply moved the teachers around to fill gaps. Garth felt more like a pawn than ever, and he wasn't even given the dignity of being told why he was being moved around.

The classes really were designed in a way that anyone could simply jump in and take over at any point in the course. All teachers were substitutes. All teachers were pawns.

Garth wondered if the pieces in a chess game ever wondered who was moving them around, who was playing, what the stakes of the game were, and if they even realized a game was happening. He wondered if this entire school system was a model to see how far they could go with running a school this way before someone pushed back.

He knew even less about English than he did about Government Studies, and for his first four periods he could do little but watch the students read. He wondered what these classes were like when Mrs. Kri was in it. He hoped they were more lively and full of actual discussion. Perhaps they were, for now, until the course became like Government Studies.

For four periods in a row, Garth occupied himself by counting the brain cells that died from inactivity. He wished he'd been given some course material to prepare for something over the weekend, but he had been given nothing. He hadn't even been told what room to report to until this morning.

He was barely coherent by the time Government Studies came around and was not in the mood for discussion on just what this country was doing in so many other nations, and how we handled ourselves while there. He still read his articles, still acted as the relay for students to discuss the topic, but he would much rather have been sleeping.

The two classes came and went, and on his way to his only remaining gym period, he swung by Mrs. Kri's room. He found the shepherd/collie behind the desk, looking just as brain dead as Garth felt.

"Hey, Sasha," Garth said from the door.

She lifted her head from the desk and faced Garth, smiling like it was the last period of Monday, "Hi, Garth."

"Sorry you got stuck with this, too."

"Oh, you had this job the first half of the day?"

"Yup. So not only are we gym coaches, we're also substitutes."

"This is nothing. One time they had me doing the chemistry classes because Jeremy was out."

"Was it just as boring?"

"It's all in the book. All in the outline."

Garth nodded. "So this is all they want from us."

"Pretty much."

Students were arriving and taking their seats.

"Catch up with you later, Ms. Grace. Bye." He waved and backed away from the door.

He changed back into his gym clothes and pretended to guide the students in badminton. Garth thought he would give up one of his testicles just to jump in and play with the students, show them how to be a team, push them to be active instead of passive, if only to have some kind of activity.

Finally the last bell rang, and Garth remained in the gym. Terrance stood by the outside door, waiting for Garth as the students gathered in front of him, expecting to go outside for lacrosse practice.

When everyone seemed to be here, and the coaches were pulling the dividers across the floor, Garth blew his whistle and raised his paws.

"Attention, everyone! I'm back. A-shift workouts report to the weight room." The students smiled, tails wagged and they ran up to Garth. He repeated himself to the other half of the room. "All A-shift workouts follow me to the weight room! We're picking up the weights again."

Terrance left the door and walked to meet him. Coach Bob, Coach Joey and Coach Paul also closed in on Garth.

"Coach Hood, what are you doing?" said Terrance.

"Doing my job."

He started walking towards the door to the weight room, all the students ran ahead of him, filtering through the divider.

"Those pups need to practice," said Joey.

"They also need to work out. That's why I was hired, and it's my job to make sure it happens. So here I am. Terrance, you can handle lacrosse by yourself. I need to be here."

"Coach Hood," said Paul, "those are my pups. If you want to take them away from me, you should talk to me first."

Garth turned to each one of them, gave them an equal share of a knifing glare. "It's Mister Hood, and maybe all of you should have talked to me before stealing my pups."

"Ms. Dover told us to make sure they have as much practice time as possible."

"And she told me it's my job to keep them on the program. Even though I'm never here, I still have to make it happen."

"Garth, you're on lacrosse duty. I need you out there with me."

"I'm staying in the weight room."

"All right," Terrance said, "fine, start the workouts again, but you're still on lacrosse duty."

"No, I'm staying in the room so nobody steals them again. If those numbers from the nurse don't go up, I'm out of a job."

Garth walked away from them.

"Coach Hood," said Terrance, "get back here."

Garth jogged, grinning, knowing they couldn't keep up with him. He ran all the way to the weight room and closed the door. Most of the students had already begun setting up their weights. Evan was in here as well, setting up the bench. He made bedroom eyes at Garth from across the room. Nobody noticed because the others were looking at the mastiff.

"What happened to you, Mister Hood?" said one of the pups.

"Why'd you close the door?"

"Hopefully it'll keep them out. And they gave me a lot of other things to do, but I decided to start doing my job again. Hurry up and start, everyone. If you're into your workouts they can't pull you away."

They spread out across the room, loaded weights on barbells, picked up dumbbells and picked up their routines where they had left off. Garth navigated the different benches and machines, observing the athletes, making sure they remembered correct form and pacing and were using the right amount of weight. Twenty minutes later, there was a knock on the door, and Garth's ears perked up.

"Don't let them take us away," Evan said from the bench press.

"Yeah, I miss working out," said one of the other dogs, snickering. "Especially with you."

Garth approached the door and opened it. Standing before him, flanked by the other four gym coaches, was a light-furred dog Garth had never seen before. He could not pin down his breed.

"Who are you?"

The thin dog looked put off, but answered in the most neutral voice Garth had ever heard. "I am Mister Croshaw, the Vice Principal."

"Oh, I think this is the first time I've ever seen you," Garth said. "How are you?"

"Indeed. An issue was brought to my attention, since Ms. Dover is out for the day, that you refuse to give the students to their coaches?"

"No."

"No, you are not refusing?"

"I mean I'm doing my job. I'm supposed to keep these students on a weightlifting program, but when I got them on a routine, the school pulled me from the room and now I hear the other coaches have stopped the workouts."

"As I understand it," said Mister Croshaw, "football and wrestling competitions begin soon and the athletes need to practice."

"They also need to be in the weight room twice a week. It's my job."

"Coach Hood—"

"Mister Hood, please."

"Yes, Mister Hood, the school needs to consider all needs of the students. As competition season is so close, it seems to me the most important thing to do is train the athletes."

"The school wants them on weights to put some mass on them in time for the competitions. Do you want that to happen?"

"Mister Hood... It is your first year teaching, am I correct?"

"If you call this teaching, yes."

"Then I'm afraid I must defer to the preferences of the other coaches. They know what is best for the athletes."

"Ms. Dover told me the numbers from the nurse were not good, so these students need to resume their workouts."

"I have faith that you can get your assigned tasks done, Mister Hood, but right now these students need to practice."

Garth almost growled at him. He almost did. He wanted to. He considered the only consequence would be termination.

"Ms. Dover told me I need to keep them on the program. Didn't she tell you the school has a weight program?"

"A weight program is vital to the school's success, Mister Hood, but so is practice before the season. The weight room will have to be on hold until the season gets underway."

"At what point will I be allowed to do my job?"

"Please, Mister Hood, be cooperative. We're all in this together."

Garth laughed from the belly, stepped aside and motioned Mister Croshaw inside.

"Then you tell them."

The canine did not move from his spot. "That is your responsibility, Mister Hood. Please allow these other coaches to do their jobs at this time. Thank you." He turned around and walked away.

The students had stopped lifting when the door opened and were now sitting on benches, leaning on racks and the other machines.

Terrance waved an arm. "Practice. Everyone."

The pups shook their heads and filed out of the room. Evan walked up next to Garth and looked up at him.

"I'll be in my office," Garth said. He stepped out of the room and followed the sideline through the gymnasium and into the locker room.

Garth sat down in the chair. He wanted to fold into himself and never step outside the box again. This place did not want him to do a good job so why should he even try? It would be so easy to slip into that again, just accept whatever they threw at him, throw his arms in the air and declare it's hopeless. Garth felt that way right now. He had nobody on his side, and yet he was still expected to make this happen. He sat still for ten minutes, rubbing his temples.

Evan peeked around the corner. Garth raised his eyes and lowered his hand.

"How long you got?" Garth said.

"Long enough to run to the bathroom."

"Perfect."

Evan stepped in, closed the door behind him and locked it as Garth opened a drawer and took out the lube. In mere seconds Evan was naked and pulling Garth's shirt over his head. Garth raised his arms and let Evan do all the work while Garth lubed himself up.

Evan felt Garth up and down, rubbed his abs, felt Garth's hips, and groped his balls while trying to wrap his fingers around Garth's bicep. While he was doing that, Garth reached behind Evan and lubed under his tail. It wagged wildly.

When Garth withdrew his finger, Evan turned around and bent over on the desk. Garth stood behind him and pushed in immediately. Evan reached back, held Garth's hand as he worked his way in.

Garth did not waste time being gentle or passionate this time. He rammed Evan hard and deep. The dobie gripped Garth's hand and braced himself on the desk for the ride. Evan had been asking Garth to go harder for a while, but Garth had been enjoying the more passionate moments, when it wasn't just a fuck. Now all of a sudden it didn't seem to matter as much. Garth gave it to him as hard as Evan wanted, and the pup grinned wider than ever.

Relieving the tension made his cock even more sensitive, and Garth couldn't stop himself from slamming him hard. Garth blew his load, and he kept thrusting. His cock was telling him it was over, he was finished, but he kept thrusting. Evan moaned and gasped and held Garth's hand tighter.

Garth didn't want to go soft. It felt too good, even now. He wished he hadn't fucked Evan so hard this time. After a dozen more thrusts, he was too soft to keep going. He stopped, sighed, and pulled out.

Evan let go of Garth's hand, turned around and leaned on the desk, looking up at Garth. The look in his eyes was delightfully evil. He reached up, felt Garth's face, and licked his muzzle a few times. Garth kissed him, held him around the waist, and squeezed his rear.

Evan's cock was between Garth's legs, lifting his balls up. Garth growled, picked Evan up under the arms and guided him to the floor. The dobie still was dreamy-eyed from being filled. His cock was all the way up. Garth grabbed the bottle again, lubed himself up, lubed

Evan's flagpole and sat down on it. He took it down halfway rather easily this time, but he still had to stop. Evan thrust, grinning. Garth gritted his teeth and took it, also smiling down at the dobie. Now he was being more passionate than aggressive.

Evan must have loved watching a muscle dog whimper from his dick, for he kissed Garth every time the mastiff whimpered, and Evan fucked him just a little less passionately.

Garth felt pulsing under his tail, and now he became dreamy-eyed. Evan was feeling Garth's chest, cupping the pecs and teasing the veins that had popped up everywhere. Garth felt Evan's chest. He liked being impaled on this branch. It had a strange appeal to it.

It was still alive. The part of him that graduated with a doctorate and still felt enthusiasm for entering the working world. It rattled the cage it was trapped in, and Garth would not force it to be quiet.

Chapter 22

Everyone was at the next Student Council, and the debate was lively. Garth did not sit behind the desk, but leaned in front of it. He wasn't just an observer injecting scripts into the debate anymore. Now he was an active part of it.

Garth hadn't touched the topics for this week's meeting at all. The council was busy debating last week's points, now with more members to get involved in the discussion. The most critical was a Golden Halo in the cafeteria. Garth kept the debate organized so it didn't degenerate into people talking over one another, and he gave them an adult mind to bounce their thoughts off of. Garth gave them real perspectives to consider, not just the script's point, and they debated that topic for half an hour by itself.

When people began repeating themselves, Garth moved them on to the topic of different assignments for the athletes. This debate took much less time. Everyone was against it, even after Garth brought the script into the discussion. Garth did not bother moving on to the final two points on the list, and with the last fifteen minutes of the session, he took a vote.

All eight students voted nay on the measure for fast food in the school.

All eight students voted nay on the special assignments for the athletes.

For the first time all school year, they had finally reached a decision on their own.

The session concluded, the students ran to the late busses, and Garth sat alone with Evan in the classroom, Garth on his desk, Evan behind his.

"Be proud," Garth said. "The school just said no to fast food."

"It seemed a lot simpler when we were all 'we just want better food.'"

"I think you deserve a reward." Garth walked to the door, shut it, turned around and pulled off his shirt. Evan smiled.

Garth tossed his shirt on the desk, held his arms up and did a double bicep pose. Evan smiled and panted.

"Is this what all senators get after voting?" said the dobie.

"Yeah." Garth switched to a side chest pose. "After a long, hard day of listening to other people talk, and then finally making a good decision, they turn off the cameras and bring the hookers in."

"And dogs like us?"

"They'd adjourn to one of the other rooms and bring the muscle dogs in."

Evan grinned, feeling himself through his pants. "What happens if they don't reach a decision?"

"Then no eye candy for them." Garth lowered his arms, flexed his chest and let his biceps push against his pecs.

"I could do this all day if I had entertainment afterwards. You should put in a job app to be an entertainer for the real senators."

Garth raised one arm and showed the abdominals and tricep. "If I knew where to put in the application."

"I thought about it a lot, and I wanna be a senator when I graduate." Evan reached into his pants, pulled his cock out and started rubbing it.

"That means getting a law degree."

"Oh, then never mind."

Garth chuckled. "Get over here."

The dobie stood, walked between the desks and stood in front of Garth as he posed. He unzipped Garth's pants, undid the clasp and pulled them down just far enough. Garth was in another front double bicep pose. Evan dropped to his knees and sucked the mastiff. Garth dropped the pose and loomed over Evan instead, flexing his chest and using his biceps to pucker it. Evan's eyes were pointed up, straining to see. He sucked harder, rubbed himself faster.

The door handle turned. Evan halted, turned his eyes to the door. Garth faced it, too. Sasha Grace peeked around the corner and stared, breathless.

Garth smiled. "It's okay. He's eighteen."

Sasha blinked a few times, then slipped back around the corner and closed the door behind her.

Evan released Garth's cock and spoke up to him. "Are we in trouble now?"

"Nah, Ms. Grace hates this place as much as I do."

"Oh." He opened his mouth and swallowed Garth's dick again. He felt Garth's abs with his other hand.

Garth began to thrust. Evan held Garth's dick with one hand and kept up with his muzzle. Garth leaned over, held Evan's head

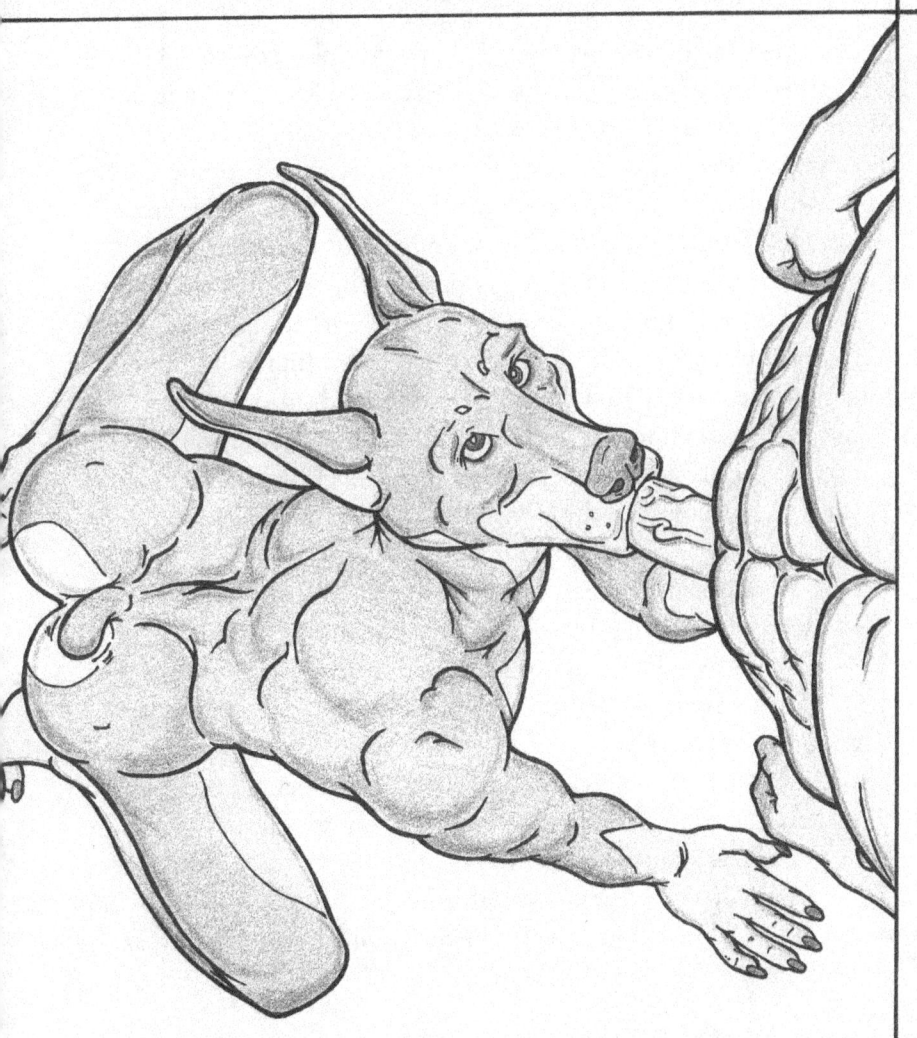

and kept thrusting. Evan still looked up at Garth, muzzle partially hidden behind his pecs. Evan smiled as Garth pushed himself down his muzzle, making his tongue work harder.

He held the back of Evan's head and fucked his muzzle. Evan realized he didn't need to work anything, just let his muzzle be the hole. Garth used it and thrust faster and faster. Evan moaned, reached behind Garth and held his rear as Garth pounded the dobie's face.

Garth thrust once. Twice. Three times, and shot his load hard. Evan gagged a little as it hit the back of his throat, but he sucked it all down. Evan continued rubbing himself, and when he couldn't get any more out of Garth, he opened his mouth and lay back on the floor. Garth knelt over him, held Evan's pole and suckled the tip as Evan rubbed faster and faster. There was a lot of pre in it, and it lubed Garth's tongue as he worked Evan's throbbing erection.

Evan now fucked Garth's face once. Twice. Thrice. Four deep thrusts as far as Garth could take them, and Evan spilled his seed against the back of Garth's throat. The mastiff took all of it.

Garth released Evan, let his dick fall back to his chest. They smiled at each other for a moment. Evan reached up, licked Garth on the muzzle once. Garth held his face, licked him back.

Moments later, fully dressed, Evan opened the door and walked out. Sasha was standing just around the corner, leaning on the wall, arms folded. Evan looked back at her, smiled, grinned, and ran down the hall. Sasha turned the corner and stood in the doorframe, facing Garth, who was still putting his shirt on.

"What the hell, Garth!"

Garth faced her, grinning. "I'm his type, and he's mine."

"That was... That was not right."

"This school isn't right. Nobody will let me do anything, so I'm doing Mister Silvers."

His shirt was finally on, and Garth walked behind the desk and gathered his things. Sasha stood still. Her mind was just as still.

"Did you want to talk to me?"

"Actually yeah. It was about this English class."

"What do you need to ask me for? I only know as much as the book says."

"I was going to ask if you wanted to work together on something. Something to make the class more interesting."

"What'd you have in mind?"

"I don't know. I was hoping you'd have an idea. I'm tired of the routine."

"So am I. I recommend finding a hot student to fuck. Its doing wonders for me."

Sasha rolled her eyes, turned around and left the classroom. Garth smiled, tail wagging, gathered the papers and walked out himself.

The next morning he dropped the Student Council's ballot in the vice principal's mailbox, and proceeded straight to English I.

According to the outline, he was supposed to go over the last chapter they read, hitting on the following eight points of theme and literary style. Garth had read the chapter himself, though he had not had time to read the previous chapters, so he would know what he was talking about.

"All right, everyone, the book wants me to examine the themes and uses of literary devices line by line in this chapter." He let the book drop flat on the desk. "Doesn't that sound like the perfect way to kill the joy of reading?"

Some of the students laughed.

"I mean it. I remember when I was in school, and the teacher would make us read a chapter, then we'd spend the next day talking about the chapter we just read. For the love of dog, can't we just read the book? Can't we just read it and enjoy it? I swear classes like this are designed to kill the joy. Forcing you to stop every ten pages and analyze and examine everything you just read kills any joy you can get from reading a good book. Am I right?"

The students nodded, laughed.

"Wait, wait, there's a reason they do this. They want to make sure you're reading the material and understanding it, but rather than invest time into earlier grades and making reading comprehension a priority, they instead force feed you all the stuff you're supposed to understand. It's not the same as understanding it yourself. So be honest. How many of you would rather just read the book, start to finish, and talk about it afterwards?"

More than half of the students raised their paws.

"I thought so. Someone who didn't raise their hands, what would you rather be doing? Yes?"

He called on one of the females in the back row, who looked like she would rather be texting.

"Why do we have to read it at all? What's the point?"

"Excellent question!" Garth said. "Why am I learning this? Why are we learning anything? Let's discuss this. How can we move on if we don't figure that part out, right?"

It was a good day, for all the classes. Garth gave them until the end of next week to read the book, and then they would discuss it. Garth promised to ignore what the script told him the book meant, what they should notice and why they should be impressed. He wanted to leave that up to the students. He was sure they would reach their own conclusion.

He was still powerless to do anything during lacrosse. He searched for a way to break out of the routine, but there were no openings so long as Terrance was around. His hour was up, and then he joined speech team, already in progress.

Garth sat in the chair at this desk. The students performed at the back of the class, with everyone facing them as they performed mismatched speeches. These were famous speeches if they were performed by someone else. Some of them Garth recognized, but most he had never heard of, and could only give feedback as a casual observer.

He thought about the next step the outline recommended and the props he would have to collect for it. He watched the vixen standing before everyone, trying to perform an ancient wartime speech from the point of view of the enemy. Garth had no idea how the enemy would perform a speech like this, but he assumed it was correct.

Next the outline specified she was supposed to perform the speech with some sort of distraction. In the past, some of the students had pretended to be crying babies, or counted backwards from one hundred very loudly. All of which were recommended by the outline, and Garth was supposed to assign them. There were still several predetermined distractions Garth had not given them: loud tapping on desks, whistling, people moving around.

Practical as they were, Garth had an idea for a real distraction. Something the students would not expect. He couldn't act worth a damn, but there was something he could do.

"All right, Lily," Garth said. "Very good. Now, perform it again normally. Be ready for distractions."

"What are we doing?" one of the dogs said.

"It'll be a surprise."

Lily began the speech from the beginning. Garth let the pen drop from his hand, stood up and began pulling his shirt off. Lily stammered for only a half second, then recovered and resumed the speech to warriors of the Bronze Age.

The other students had turned in their chairs to see what Garth was doing. Some grinned, others shied away, and others clapped and laughed. Lily gave a rousing wartime speech to her soldiers, telling them it was time for battle and it was their duty to die for the glory of the king.

Garth set his shirt on the teacher's desk and wandered between the desks.

"Someone give me a beat!"

Every student pulled out their cell phones and scrolled through their music. The first song to emerge had a beat, and Garth moved to it, moving his body like he knew Evan would enjoy.

The laughter drowned out all but the baseline of the song, and Garth danced around the classroom, moving his body like his rent depended on it. Out of the corner of his eye he caught a few pairs of eyes looking in through the window panel in the door, and then slinking away.

Lily kept it up. She told her warriors to steel themselves and remember what the enemy will do to their wives and daughters if they should show cowardice in battle, and what the gods would do to them in the next life should they die without having first taken one of the enemy down.

Garth joined her at the back of the class and shook his hips and bounced his pecs, never touching her, making yapping gestures with his hands, pointing at the audience, miming a yawn. The speech team students clapped, whistled, cheered. Some hid their faces, giggling and embarrassed.

Finally, Lily finished the speech and took a bow. Garth took a bow with her, and applauded for her.

"Very good," Garth said. "Very good! I didn't think you'd make it. I was really trying."

"That was awful, Mister Hood!" Lily shouted, bending at the knees laughing.

"Hey, I can't act! But I can shake it! Kill the beat."

The music went silent.

"New song, please. Who's next?"

A new song started up from someone else's phone. One of the males rose from his seat and took to the front of the class. Garth began gyrating around the classroom.

On Friday morning, Garth sat opposite Ms. Dover, who looked at him sternly, but still professionally.

"Mister Hood, I have received word that you have not been using the scripts for Student Council."

"I've been letting the students debate."

"I have been instructed to give this to you." She slid a paper up to Garth. It was another list of points for the council to debate. "Please note the updated scripts and make sure the council hears them."

Garth glanced at the points. They were identical to the ones from a week before, but the scripts were longer. He zeroed in on the longest paragraph.

2. If the school should consider installing a Golden Halo restaurant in its cafeteria instead of the cafeteria staff / *Students should consider revenue benefits to the school. Montgomery High will receive up to 15% of gross revenue, which will help to reduce taxes on the community and provide greater freedom for the school to purchase supplies and improve equipment. Students are also encouraged to consider the cost of labor of running a cafeteria, materials billed directly to the school, and the cost of maintaining the equipment. Students are encouraged to consider impact on their fellow students in terms of quality of school lunch. Surveys indicate the majority of students are dissatisfied with their cafeteria, both in terms of choices, and taste. Other studies*

from various school districts that have implemented a similar program show a significant increase in approval on both counts.

Garth turned his muzzle up to Ms. Dover again and smiled. "So someone *is* paying attention to the votes. I was wondering."

"Please, Mister Hood, make sure the students are aware of the issue. If you are not following your scripts—"

"I am bringing it up, but I'm also giving the pups an adult's perspective. You wanted me to do that, didn't you?"

"Your job is to moderate, using the script as a guide, Mister Hood. Please do so at this time."

"So because they didn't vote the way the script was leading them, I must not be doing my job? I'm not here to lead the students to one conclusion. I'm there to help them understand the issue."

"It would be a very good thing if the students understood what was going to happen, Mister Hood."

"Oh? Why do you say that?"

"What I mean to say is that the students need to understand why this is being done."

Garth nodded. "So the decision's already been made. When's it going to happen?"

"I cannot comment on that, Mister Hood. All I can say is that this is a decision that impacts a lot of people, and the students need to realize that."

"I knew it. Someone already made the choice. Way to show them how democracy works."

"Mister Hood, I was under the impression you would be more open to new ways of doing things."

"I'll make sure the council knows exactly why this is happening. Do you have anything else for me?"

"Yes, I have received reports of inappropriate behavior during speech team rehearsal."

Garth grinned. His tail thumped the back of the chair. "The outline called for a distraction. The students were used to all the distractions in the outline, so I gave them a new one."

"You took off your shirt and did a striptease in the classroom."

"Only the shirt. Just enough to be funny."

"Mister Hood, I shouldn't need to tell you that was uncalled for. Please stick to the outline provided for you."

Garth grinned wider. "You jealous they got to see it and not you?"

Ms. Dover cleared her throat. "It has also come to my attention you are being uncooperative with the other coaches?"

"You told me it was my job to get those students on weights. So when I tried, Paul, Terrance, Joey and Bob went to the vice principal, and he told me weight room wasn't as important as practice. He basically put a stop to the weight program. Can you help me?"

"Mister Croshaw is very experienced, Mister Hood. He knows what he's doing."

Garth closed his eyes and took a breath. "I'll say it again. I cannot do the job you hired me for if the vice principal himself won't let me. Will you go to Mister Croshaw and explain to him there is a weight program, I am in charge of it, and I need to be allowed to do my job?"

"Mister Hood, resources are tight, at this time. I'll talk to him. We'll see what happens."

"We'll see what happens? We'll see? The job you hired me to do, and the best you can do is we'll see? If the numbers from the nurse come back bad again, don't blame me. I have been trying to do my job for weeks, and it won't be my fault if there are no results."

"That is all I can promise at this time, Mister Hood."

"Fine by me," Garth stood up and turned to leave.

"Make sure to fill the soda machines before you leave tonight, Mister Hood."

Garth walked out of the office. When he was in the halls, he growled, crumpling the paper in one hand. He pulled out his phone, checked the time. Five minutes to eight, plenty of time. He took a detour, veered off and poked his head into a particular classroom. It was Evan's homeroom, and the dobie sat on the opposite side of the room.

"Mister Silvers," Garth said from the door.

Evan looked up, smiled when he saw Garth.

Garth looked at the old canine at the desk. Garth wasn't sure what his name was. He had never had occasion to speak with this teacher before. "Excuse me. I need to borrow Mister Silvers."

The old canine nodded and waved to Evan. Evan waved back, picked up his backpack and walked to the door. He walked side by side with Garth down the hall. They were both hard already.

"What happened?" Evan said.

"I'll tell you later. This time I want you in me. I need it to get through today."

Evan grinned. "Sure."

Five minutes later, in Garth's tiny office, the mastiff was naked and bent over the desk, the dobie more than halfway buried in him. Garth held his muzzle closed and tried not to scream, but he grunted pretty heavy from time to time. Evan pulled out, shoved himself back in, going a little deeper every time. Garth was determined to take the whole thing, and a Friday was the perfect day to do it.

This time Evan held Garth's shoulders and pulled Garth back as he pushed himself forward. Garth got that upsetting feeling in his gut again.

"Uuuuggghhhhh, how far is it?"

"Thee-quarters."

"So close. So fucking close. Just give me the rest."

"You sure?"

"Fuck yes, make balls touch so I can be gay all day."

Evan giggled, pulled out, shoved it back in. Garth gritted his teeth, willing his body to accept the intruder. Evan worked it in gradually, but still aggressively. Garth held the sides of the desk and hoped it would be over soon, and wished it would never end.

Garth was doing a very bad job keeping quiet. He couldn't help it. It hurt so good, and it hit all the right places every time the pup pushed in deeper than before.

Evan shoved himself in. Garth felt like the pup had poked a hole in his stomach and he almost begged him to stop, but the mastiff held his muzzle shut and let the pup do his thing.

Evan pulled out and thrust six more times, going a little deeper into the bigger dog each time. Garth growled and moaned and panted. Evan was rubbing Garth's back. Some veins must have popped out.

Evan paused. Garth hung his head and panted. "How far?"

"About three-quarters."

"Fuck! Has anyone else been able to take this?"

"A couple pups."

"What?!"

"I was with this cat last year. He'd heard about me and wanted to see it. So he came to my house and I showed him. Just minutes later he was on his back begging me to give it all to him. I did. Oh yeah, he'd been with others, and he took it all. Didn't take long either."

"What was his secret?"

"I don't know. It was like his ass was made for huge dicks."

"Damn it, I can't let a teenager beat me! Make it fit!"

The gut-moving feeling was easier to deal with now. Garth smiled at himself as Evan drilled deeper and deeper. He gripped the desk as Evan pushed harder. It was working. He had pushed past a limit. A few thrusts later, he felt Evan's hips touching his.

"You did it, Garth!" Evan said. "You're finally gay!"

"Fuck! Finally! Thank you, Evan! You about finished?!"

Evan giggled, squeezed Garth's shoulders. "Wimping out on me already?"

"Hell yeah!"

"You're in luck. I'm almost there."

Evan pumped Garth deep. It felt so good to feel Evan against him like this. Evan felt close, intimate. As soon as Garth had the thought, Evan pulled all the way out, and then plunged back in. Garth sprawled out, stretched his arms and growled. Garth finished as well, all over the desk.

"Wow…" Garth said.

"Hey, look at that. I'm still not done."

Garth laughed. "Ugh… hurry up."

"Do I hear a please?"

"Don't forget whose bigger, puppy. But yes, please finish. I'm gay enough for one day."

"Oh, all right."

Evan giggled again and thrust a few more times, shallow at first, and then deep. It lasted well into first period.

Chapter 23

The weather was getting cold, and Garth wondered how the school expected them to make a lacrosse team in winter, when they had to be inside.

The students were running, they were passing, and some of them were actually catching, but according to the course outline, everyone should be proficient enough to be a coordinated team by now. Garth couldn't imagine them coordinating a song, let alone a lacrosse game.

Garth was squatting over the grass, arms on his thighs, watching the athletes run around trying to act as a team. The outline had them learn basic formations, interceptions, and how to be available when needed. The outline had run them through so much Garth had a difficult time believing the students were not a coordinated team by now, but if they didn't even have the foundation of catching and passing, the rest would not follow.

The aspiring physicist turned his head to face the aspiring anthropologist, who stood about twenty feet away, also watching the students. Garth was sure the other mastiff had gained weight.

It was a strange problem. He and Terrance could do better than this, but if they actually did use the outline to turn these students into a good lacrosse team, that would tell the higher-ups this course outline worked, and it would expedite the gradual replacement of teachers with interns. In a way, Terrance's attitude was an act of rebellion. On the surface it seemed like laziness, but in a way, Garth wanted to join the protest.

He wished the pups didn't have to suffer in order for there to be a protest, and Garth also thought that was giving the fat mastiff too much credit. He couldn't tell the difference between trying to sabotage the direction things were going, and just being too lazy to get up and do something about it. Garth loathed living in a world where the two were interchangeable.

He had had a great day until lacrosse practice. He'd had time to read through the book his English classes were reading, and started great conversations with his English students for all four periods. Most seemed much happier to read the book and then discuss it at the end, instead of stopping every chapter and analyzing it to death. It gave them a chance to decide for themselves what they thought of it, instead of a teacher telling them what they should think, and Garth enjoyed all of that.

Government Studies was going very well, too. The articles the students had brought were interesting, and they made Garth think on his feet. He was no political expert, but just from doing the class this way he felt like he was actually qualified to be there.

The textbook lessons were boring and uninteresting, and Garth felt bad for assigning them as homework every night on top of finding articles to discuss, but it had been worth it.

He had found his own way to teach the classes, and it was working. Garth was happy on the job, and he was starting to enjoy this. For the first time since he arrived, he felt he was connecting with the students at last. There were plenty of lazy dogs who just wanted to spend the whole period texting, but connecting with the six or eight students who wanted to be challenged made the whole thing worth it.

Then he came here, and he was powerless to challenge these students. All he could do was squat and wait for the period to end. Garth agreed with Terrance's passive protest, whether that was the intent or not, but he did not agree with the method. If it were up to Garth, he would find his own way to make these students into a lacrosse team.

He did not meet Evan after school. They had already arranged it so if Garth did not come back to his office by a certain time, Evan should go home. Garth needed a break, and he hoped Evan needed one, too.

On Tuesday, he continued the discussion where each individual class left off from English through Government Studies. His programming class was exhausting. He was starting to get the hang of it, but before he could practice anything on his own, he had to grade a student who had just finished the project and was now starting on the next one early.

He joined his students for speech team. When he walked in, the students in the audience cheered and hollered. The dog giving the speech did not falter his lines, which was a good sign.

"Sorry, puppies and kitties. No show from me today. Ms. Dover had a talk with me, and it seems someone complained about my dance moves the other week."

Everyone laughed.

"Show of hands, who here was offended by the distraction?"

Nobody raised a paw. The dog still gave his speech.

"I thought so. All right, they have a problem with me taking my shirt off, how 'bought this. I'll just roll up my sleeves real casual, like this. Who wants to arm-wrestle?"

To Garth's surprise, there were volunteers. He got a strange scent from some of the males in the group. He wondered how many of them had been with Evan at some point in the past.

Garth had enjoyed watching these students go from uncertain teenagers to confident actors in the short time he had been here. He was glad to play some part in it instead of following an educator's outline.

Wednesday was a wonderful repeat of Tuesday and Monday, and this time he looked forward to staying after school.

Garth leaned in front of the desk in his Government Studies room and waited for the pups to enter. The eight arrived, took their usual seats, and Garth held the paper with the different points in front of him.

"Happy all of you came, because I have a special treat for you. Someone heard your votes on fast food in the cafeteria."

Everyone smiled and laughed.

"Wait, wait, here's what they did. They sent me this," he turned the paper to face them, and then held it back so he could read it. He didn't need to read it. He had read it so many times he almost had it memorized. "I'll cut straight to that point first. Here's what they wrote. Students should consider revenue benefits to the school. Montgomery High will receive up to fifteen percent of gross revenue, which will help to reduce taxes on the community and provide greater freedom for the school to purchase supplies and improve equipment. Students are also encouraged to consider the cost of labor of running a cafeteria, materials billed directly to the school, and the cost of maintaining the equipment. Students are encouraged to consider impact on their fellow students in terms of quality of school lunch. Surveys indicate the majority of students are dissatisfied with their cafeteria, both in terms of choices, and taste. Other studies from various school districts that have implemented a similar program show a significant increase in approval on both counts."

Garth lowered the page and scanned the class as he spoke. "Anyone recognize what just happened?"

"They want us to change our vote?" Gina said.

"Exactly! Someone didn't like how the votes went, and they want you to reconsider because—"

As Garth spoke, the handle on the door turned. Garth paused and faced the door, and in walked Mister Croshaw, dressed as professionally and immaculately as ever.

"Oh, Mister Croshaw!" Garth said, grinning. "Nice of you to stop by and see democracy in action."

He was closing the door behind him, smiling professionally as well. "Thank you, Mister Hood. I thought I'd come back and check in on how things are going."

"Great, have a seat, listen in."

"Actually, I would like to take this moment to address the senate."

Garth pushed off the desk and stood against the other wall instead. "Of course, say all you like."

The vice principal took Garth's place in front of the desk and observed the students, never losing his generic, professional smile.

"I read your votes, and I must say I have a feeling all of you are not getting the full picture. To address the entirety of the point Mister Hood was making, I want all of you to think very hard about how this will impact your school. Now, it won't matter much to you seniors, but in a democracy, it's important to think how your choices will impact those who come after you are gone.

"I also want to stress that the school has a vested interest in making sure the students are well provided for, and that everyone's needs are met fairly and responsibly. Montgomery High is committed to providing a good education for all students, and a good meal between classes is essential to that commitment."

"I want everyone to understand that the school is facing a huge budget shortfall, and if it is not reconciled quickly, we may lose yet more funding. As a result, and to achieve our commitment, it is our duty to ensure we are providing you with the best quality we can in all areas of education."

"I want all of you to consider the people who will be impacted the most by your decision: the students who will come after you. Budget cuts are only looking to get worse, and if we cannot provide a good meal for the students by our own means, we owe it to them to turn to the people who can."

"This decision requires very little of us. In fact, it will close the budget shortfall, and maybe even allow the school to turn a profit, allowing us to redirect those funds to improving other aspects of the education experience. All of you are too young to understand exactly what all of this means, but trust me when I say we are all very excited by this proposal. We hope you will join us in helping us realize our goal of providing the best education possible for our students. And as a special thank-you for listening, I have with me gift cards," he reached into his pocket and removed eight gift cards colored with a glowing golden halo over a hamburger, "each worth ten dollars. Please keep everything I said in mind when making your decision."

He walked to each desk and passed them out. The students picked them up, smiled and fidgeted with them. Mister Croshaw walked back to the desk and motioned for Garth to take the floor.

Garth busted out laughing and walked back to his place. He reached out and held Mister Croshaw around the shoulder, pulling the dog right up to his side, laughing so hard he could barely stand.

"Thank you, Mister Croshaw!" he said when he could finally speak. "Thank you for showing us how democracy works! And for presenting the issue as a matter of bettering our children's education instead of a matter of profit for a tiny group of people we will never see."

He slapped the vice principal on the back, nearly knocking him to the floor. Mister Croshaw's professional posture wavered, and his smile fell. Garth now addressed the eight students.

"Now when you vote, if any of you vote against it, you will be portrayed as being against better education! Everybody thank our vice principal for the lobbying, thank him for all but confirming that the decision has already been made, and it is our duty to convince others why we're going along with it. Yes, thank you, Mister Croshaw! Thank you! Now, let's discuss—"

"Coach Hood."

Garth held his shoulder tighter, pulling him closer and turned his muzzle to face the vice principal. He was nose to nose with the dog. "My name is Mister Hood, please."

The students giggled.

"A word with you in the hall."

Garth released him. Mister Croshaw straightened his overcoat, walked to the door and opened it, gesturing for Garth to leave.

The mastiff handed the paper to Evan and turned to the rest of the students. "Evan will moderate while I'm gone. I suggest you start discussing the second point now, since our vice principal has shown just how important it is."

Garth walked out the door. Mister Croshaw followed, and closed it behind him.

"Mister Hood, that was uncalled for."

"You walk into my senate, misrepresent the issue and bribe the senators. You might have changed somebody's life just now."

"Your job is to help the students come to the best decision possible. I have observed you deviating from the scripts and misguiding the students."

"What difference does it make? None of their votes matter. None of this is going to change anything. The school will have fast food for lunch and that's that. When's it gonna happen, next year, next semester?"

"This is your final warning, Mister Hood. If there is another violation of school policy, you will be terminated. Remember you are a gym coach. You are replaceable."

"I am a physicist. I am an English teacher. I am a weight room instructor. I am moderator of student council. I am enriched computer programming instructor. I do an awful lot for a gym coach's pay. Speaking of that, have you or Ms. Dover talked to the other coaches about getting the athletes back on weights?"

"I or Ms. Dover will have a word with them tomorrow morning. In the meantime, Mister Hood, please do your job."

"I'm trying to do my job, but nobody will let me."

"I have faith in you, Mister Hood. I know you can turn this around at this time."

"Do you talk like this at home, too? Must be a real mood killer with the wife."

Mister Croshaw walked past Garth and down the hall to the offices. Garth smiled, opened the door and joined the council. Discussion was going strong, and Garth planned to use both hours again. Garth looked at Evan. Evan gave Garth that look, too. He had a feeling he would give another show after the cameras turned off.

Chapter 24

Today was a good day. Everything was going his way. The students were happy and engaged, he felt like he was getting into this whole teaching thing, and he had a cute pup to fuck if something bad happened, so he felt like a teenager, immune to everything.

Today was another lacrosse day, but as Garth stepped into the gymnasium and walked down the sidelines through the dividers, he resolved to leave Terrance's method of fighting the system to Terrance. He wouldn't let the pups skate by just to prove the outlines didn't work.

Coach Bob stood off to the side as two students wrestled on the mats. Evan was wrestling a dog twice his size, and somehow Evan was winning. Garth smirked, thinking he wouldn't be surprised if Evan had fucked that dog so he was letting Evan win. The fat fox noticed Garth approaching and shifted his weight from one foot to the other.

"Coach Bob. Did Ms. Dover or Mister Croshaw have a chat with you today?"

"No. Why?"

"They didn't see you?"

"No. Haven't heard from them."

"Why am I not surprised?"

"Uh?"

"No really, why did I think they would? Why did I let myself believe they'd actually talk to you?"

Bob blinked.

"All right, look coach, I'm supposed to keep the students on a weight program. It's my job, they left it to me to figure out how to make it happen, and I'm making it happen."

"Geeze. Didn't you hear Mister Croshaw the first time? It's over, Garth. Let it go."

"I can't let it go. It's my job."

"They won't do anything to you. Just forget it."

"I don't want to forget it!"

"Just leave." Bob turned away, pretended to watch the two students wrestle.

Garth blew his whistle, held up his arms, flexing his muscles for everyone to see. The students stopped and faced Garth. Evan licked his lips. So did a couple other students, which Garth thought was weird at first until he figured most of them had probably been with Evan.

"You're supposed to be in the weight room. I'm supposed to have all of you on a weight program. It's actually my job, but I haven't been allowed to do it. So I'll leave it up to all of you. How many of you enjoyed working out with me?"

All but a couple students raised their paws.

"How many of you would rather be in there right now training with me, as opposed to being here watching each other wrestle?"

Nobody raised their paws.

"Sounds great! Follow me. We'll get a quick routine in, and then the rest of the day will be wrestling practice."

The wrestling students led Garth to the weight room, leaving Bob standing alone at the mat.

Garth was last to enter the weight room, and he closed the door behind him. This would not stop anyone from entering and taking his students away, but it made him feel more secure.

"Thanks, everyone," Garth said as he removed his shirt. "I'm glad people out there want me to do a good job. I'm falling behind on my own routine, so today I'll do an upper body workout with you. All of you get back on your routines."

The students seemed suspiciously delighted, fanned out across the weight room and hopped on the equipment. Evan kept a discreet distance, which Garth was glad for. Garth loaded the barbell. The students watched, eager to see their coach bench press.

"So what happened while I've been gone?" Garth said to everyone.

"They took us out off weights a couple weeks after you were gone," said one of the canines.

"We were like, what? You got us started and now you want us to quit?"

"Just when I was starting to get to like it, they pull us out."

"What did they tell you I was doing?" Garth said as he lay on the bench. Evan casually walked to the spotter's perch and grinned down at the mastiff.

Evan leaned down and whispered in Garth's ear. "I've fucked all but one of the dogs in here."

Garth tried not to smile back.

"They told us you got us started, and now it was our job to stay on the program."

"They told you that?" Garth said. "They made it your job to figure out how to stay on the program? When did they expect you to do that?"

Someone else answered Garth. "Coach Bob said we could all find some time to come in and work out on our own."

"I shouldn't be surprised by now," said the mastiff.

He gripped the barbell, was about to lift it off, when the door opened. Garth turned his head to face the entrance. Standing there was Mister Croshaw. Garth sighed, swung his legs off the bench and sat up facing the vice principal.

"Nice to see you again, Mister Croshaw," said Garth. "Got more gift cards for us?"

"I told you, Mister Hood. Practice is a priority. Taking the students away from their practice is not good for them at this time."

"Do you want me to keep them on weights or not?"

"It is understood that the students will follow the weight routines if given the freedom to do so on their own."

"When are they supposed to do that?"

"The room is always open."

"They have practice. They have classes. I should have known you'd do something like that. You did it to me, why not everyone?"

"It is practice time, Mister Hood. The students belong there. Using school time for this purpose is not an efficient use of resources."

Garth growled, stood up and walked up to the dog. "I am fucking sick of this place! Do you want me to do my job or not?! I've been putting up with your shit for months and I'm tired of pretending to be a teacher! What the fuck do you people want?!"

"Mister Hood... I get the feeling you are agitated at this time."

"Will you please talk to me instead of spitting out that formal bullshit!"

Mister Croshaw did not speak, but moved backwards as Garth closed the distance, keeping Garth about two paces away from him. Garth noticed Evan had migrated around to his line of sight, drinking in the sight of Garth standing bare-chested, waving his arms around, and doing everything possible except lay a finger on the vice principal.

"I came here eager to do the best job I can, but every time I try, I get pushed back down! I'm going insane in these fucking classes and if I don't find a better way to teach them I'll snap! Student council is actually making decisions now, the students in English are enjoying the book, and government is full of discussion! Please fucking let me do my goddamned job!"

Garth had backed the vice principal up against the wall. The room was silent. Garth's muscles had a post-workout pump just from yelling. He was huge, veins were visible all over him, and he was nearly naked and showing it off to everyone. The other students were huddled against the wall, trying to get a better look at Garth.

"Mister Hood..." said the vice principal. "I think you should join me in my office, at this time."

Garth growled. The growl rose to a snarl, and Garth reached over, picked up a one-hundred-pound plate and chucked it across the weight room. It wobbled over the benches and crashed through the window and into the courtyard. Iron clanged on cement and wobbled to a stop. Cold air blew in through the shattered window. Garth turned, faced Mister Croshaw and snarled at him. The smaller dog tried to melt through the wall.

The mastiff came back to himself, straightened up and looked around. Evan had a massive hard-on, easily visible through his wrestling uniform. A couple of the larger jocks noticed it, groped Evan in full view of everyone, elbowing one another and grinning. A few others were winking at Garth. The leering of the students made him more uncomfortable than the panic scent coming from Mister Croshaw.

Chapter 25

Garth sat opposite Ms. Dover's desk, arms in his lap, biceps puckering his chest muscles out, but he was wearing a normal shirt so they weren't so obvious this time. He had been in suspense all day, waiting for the axe to drop, knowing they would wait until after school to do it so they could squeeze one more day of work out of him.

The poodle sat straight as a pole, reading from a paper.

"The following points have been brought before us, Mister Garth Hood. These points are..."

Mister Croshaw was standing against the wall, pretending to look at the wall instead of the mastiff in the chair.

"...failure to deliver on expectations regarding the school's new weight lifting program. Failure to effectively guide student council. Failure to adhere to guidelines while teaching Government Studies, and English I. Insubordination. Failure to adhere to hierarchy. Inappropriate behavior during speech team rehearsal. Damage to school property, which will be deducted from your final paycheck."

She now looked at Garth.

"Do you object to any of these points, Mister Hood?"

"All of them. I tried to do my job. I tried to give those pups good classes. I tried everything I could to be a good teacher. Why am I being punished for that?"

Ms. Dover looked at the paper again. "These issues have come to our attention, and due to the number and severity of them, we have decided, at this time, to let you go. Note that this will reflect on your employment record, and it not advisable to use this school as a reference for future employment."

"I wish I'd done more," Garth said.

"Well, the good news is that if you fill out this voluntary resignation form, you can avoid this going on your record."

Garth knew this was coming. There was no honor in being fired. None at all. All future employers would see was insubordination and failure to, failure to, failure to. There was no room for explanation. It was the final insult—the proof he had no voice and there was no way out of this system. They had him from all angles, and nothing would change by him getting fired from his first teaching position.

Garth took the paper and the pen and signed the form. Ms. Dover took the termination notice and fed it through the shredder. Garth had to take it completely on their word that it was the only copy.

"I'm sorry to lose you, Garth," Ms. Dover said. "You could have been a real asset to the school."

"I was. Just not the asset the school really wanted."

"Your antagonistic attitude is what did you in. Had you been more willing to cooperate, it might not have come to this."

"Why do I bother trying to explain myself?" Garth stood up. "Find some other intern to get the students on weights. See if you have better results."

"Have a nice day, Garth," Ms. Dover said. "And good luck."

"You too."

Garth walked across the school, into the locker room and stopped in his office. Evan was leaning against the wall.

"Well?" said the dobie.

"I'm fired. Though they let me quit instead so it looks better to the next place I apply."

"That sucks."

Garth opened drawers and gathered what few things he kept in his desk.

"No loss. No loss at all. Damn, I needed the money, but I'm glad it's over. Maybe the next place will actually let me do my job."

Evan hung his head. Garth rose from the desk and looked at him. He smiled. "You said you had a bus pass?"

Evan nodded.

"Gimmie your phone."

Evan reached into his pocket, handed Garth his phone, and Garth typed out a text message.

"That's my address. Swing by any time."

He gave the phone back. Evan slipped it back in his pocket.

"We'll miss you," said the doberman.

"I'll miss the students. Once they were engaged, they were great. I won't miss this place though. See ya 'round, Mister Silvers."

Garth walked by him, carrying an armful of papers and folders, by the showers, and into the pool. The pool instructors were on the sidelines, helping guide the swim teams through paces. Sasha Grace noticed Garth, stood up, and walked to meet him. Garth stopped and let her come up to him.

"Garth, that was stupid of you."

"What did you hear?"

"You assaulted the vice principal."

Garth laughed. "Don't believe what you hear. I got fired because they wouldn't let me do my job, and when I tried, they told me to stop. I'm through with this place. I guess I'm just not the kind of teacher they want."

Sasha shook her head. "I wish I could do what you did, Garth. I really do. But I need the money too much."

"And that's why things don't change. Bye, Sasha. Was good to know someone was on my side around here."

Sasha smiled, and shook her head.

Garth leaned close. "I meant what I said. Find a hot student and fuck the hell out of her. Might inspire you to do great things."

"Garth... Goodbye."

He smiled. "Bye."

He walked out of the pool, into the hall and to the nearest exit. He crossed the parking lot, walked up to his car and opened the driver's door, tossed the papers on the passenger seat and climbed behind the steering wheel. He slammed the door and was about to turn the key when an arm wrapped around his neck.

"Gotya!"

Garth gasped for a second, then leaned forward and easily broke the grip. "Evan!"

The dobie was climbing between the seats, pushed all the papers off the passenger side and sat down in it, buckling up.

"You should lock your doors. This neighborhood isn't very safe."

"You're the first one to break in."

"I am?" Evan grinned up at him.

Garth smiled. He wanted to mention how stupid this was, that someone could have seen him. Now he was driving off together and they'd know something is wrong, but instead he reached over, gripped Evan's muzzle, and shook it around playfully. Evan smiled, pretended to struggle. Garth released him and turned the key.

"Evan…" Garth took a deep breath. "I think I owe you my life."

"You can make it up to me."

"How?"

"Letting me stay the weekend."

Garth looked at the dobie and smiled. "I'll take you to the gym, and then dinner. We'll see what happens after that."

"Sure Garth. I still got this." He reached into his pocket, pulled out a small wallet and removed a Golden Halo gift card from it.

Garth laughed and snatched it from Evan's paw. "Give me that!" He rolled down the window a crack and slipped the card through it. It clacked on the asphalt and Garth rolled up the window again. "Don't touch that. It's bribe money. I expect you to stay on student council Evan, no matter who they get to run it. Vote against the script no matter what. Make things hell for them."

Evan grinned. "Are you bribing me now?"

"They can why can't I? And I mean a real dinner at my place, a good, post-workout dinner. Then you can tell me what the hell you did to the pups in this school."

Evan was still grinning at him. "I like all of those ideas."

Garth smiled, put the car in reverse and backed out of the parking spot and drove to the main road. He stopped at the intersection, looked both ways, and glanced one last time at Montgomery High in the rearview mirror. That was how he preferred to remember it.

The End

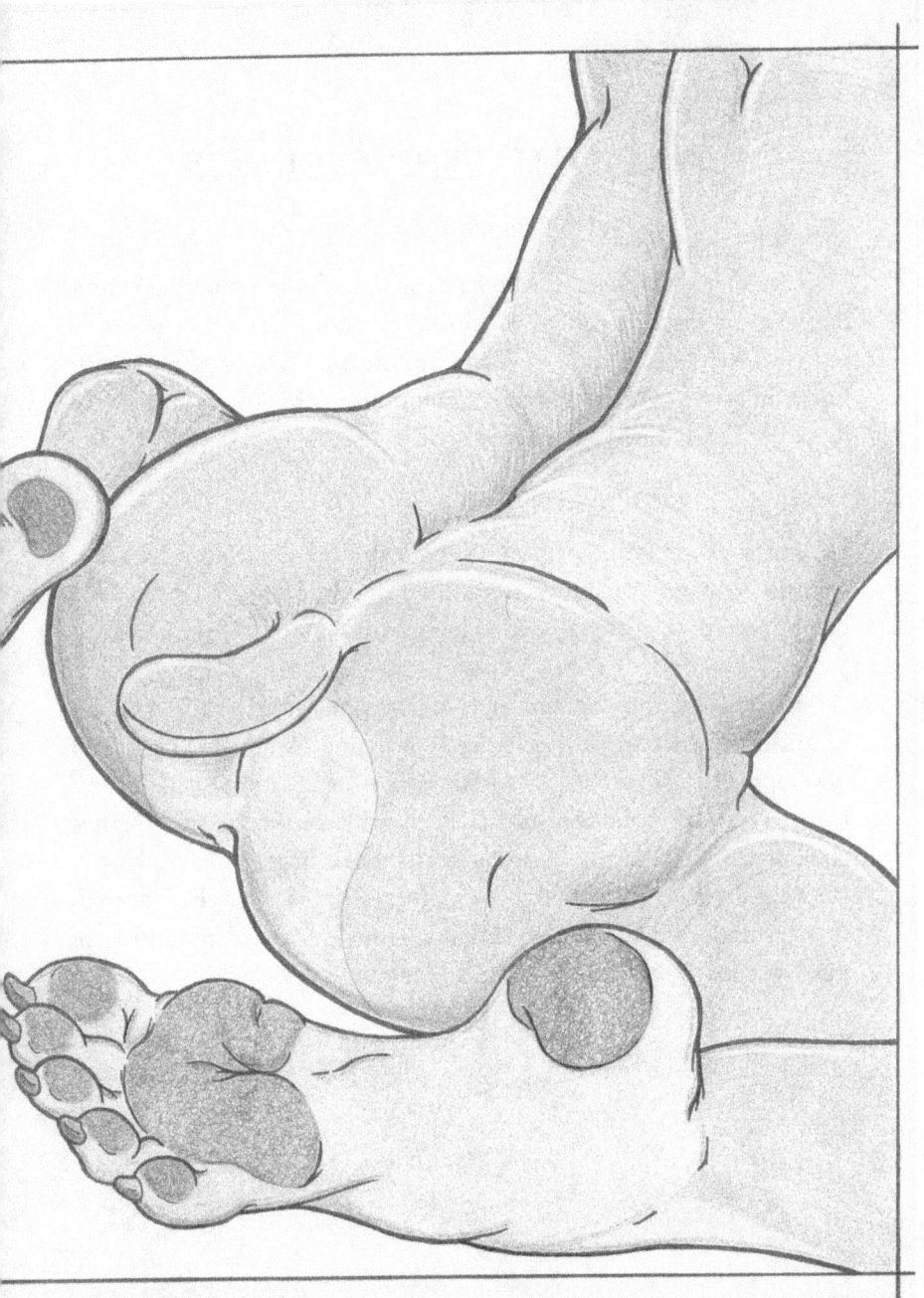

About the Artists

<u>Linkin Monroe</u>

Linkin is a Doberman who currently resides in Utah. He enjoys drawing all sorts of things, including canines, felines and equines, but he doesn't discriminate. When he isn't busy drawing, you might find him at the gym, hiking or rock climbing or hoarding underwear in a little cubby he hides under his bed.

<u>Nudog</u>

Furry erotic visual artist NuDog, has been creating works and sharing them with the furry community since the late 1990s, working on paper with traditional media: pencil, inks, graphite, markers, and paint.

Each drawing produced by NuDog is a visual representation of an imagined narrative or story (consisting of detailed character development). NuDog draws inspiration for creating visual works from erotic furry fiction and is keenly interested in the creative challenge of bringing an author's words to life in graphical form.

NuDog's favourite subject matter is the very well-endowed, or over-endowed male form, ranging from the visual rendering of massive muscle-bound studs, to cute trim twinks.

About the Author

<u>Tagenar</u>
Tagenar is a fox living in the American Midwest. He loves you, but you can't have him because that would be creepy.

Very rarely does he sit down and write a story like the one you hold in your paws, but once in a while he gets an itch that can't be scratched in any other way. Check out his other stories on SoFurry and Fur Affinity as Tagenar.

About the Publisher

<u>FurPlanet Productions</u>
FurPlanet is a small press publisher serving the niche market that is furry fiction. We sell furry-themed books and comics published by us and most major publishers in the community. If you can't get to a furry convention where we are selling in the dealers room, visit www. FurPlanet.com to shop online.

www.ingramcontent.com/pod-product-compliance
Lightning Source LLC
Chambersburg PA
CBHW051828020726
47502CB00005B/1684